For Matrimonial Purposes

Kavita Daswani was born in Hong Kong, to parents who had emigrated from India. She left school before taking her A-levels and began working as a freelance journalist. She lived in Paris and London before returning to Hong Kong, where she became fashion editor of the South China Morning Post. She was also a fashion contributor to CNN International and CNBC Asia. Kavita Daswani now lives just outside Los Angeles, with her husband and infant son.

For Matrimonial Purposes

Kavita Daswani

HarperCollins *Publishers* India

a joint venture with

New Delhi

HarperCollins *Publishers* **India**
a joint venture with
The India Today Group
by arrangement with
HarperCollins *Publishers* Limited

First published in India in 2003 by
HarperCollins *Publishers* India

Second impression 2004

Published in 2003 by
HarperCollins *Publishers* Limited

HarperCollins *Publishers*
1A Hamilton House, Connaught Place, New Delhi 110 001, India
77-85 Fulham Palace Road, London W6 8JB, United Kingdom
Hazelton Lanes, 55 Avenue Road, Suite 2900, Toronto, Ontario M5R 3L2
and 1995 Markham Road, Scarborough, Ontario M1B 5M8, Canada
25 Ryde Road, Pymble, Sydney, NSW 2073, Australia
31 View Road, Glenfield, Auckland 10, New Zealand
10 East 53rd Street, New York NY 10022, USA

Printed and bound at
Thomson Press (India) Ltd.

To Mummy and Papa,
for teaching me humor and humility.

To Sunita, Ranju, Sanam, Mansha and Sohana,
a family that I am profoundly proud to be a part of.

And especially to my exceptional husband Nissim,
who made me believe that my words have worth, and
our gorgeous son Jahan, who moved me to write as
he lay in my belly. As long as I have you both,
my life is blessed.

Thank you, Karl and Soyo, for convincing me that this story should be told. To Janine, for sitting with me in the FCC on those countless afternoons and helping me to map it out. To Susan and Fionnuala for making me think: 'Gosh, I wish I could write like that.' To Tara, for her truly heartfelt good wishes, always. To Orrin and Mini for putting up with me, goading me on, forcing me to make this happen. To Sally, for saying, memorably: 'Find the man, and that will be the key.' To Alessandra, Kim and Anna Dora, for reading to me, and letting me read to them. And to Michael, without whom there would be no happy ending. I thank my agent, Jodie Rhodes, for her scruples, integrity and passion, and Jenny Meyer for taking this to the world. And my absolute gratitude to Susan Watt and everyone at HarperCollins UK for the kindnesses they have continued to show me, every step of the way.

PART ONE

Chapter One

The normal religious marriage was and still is arranged
by the parents of the couple, after much consultation,
and the study of omens, horoscopes and auspicious
physical characteristics ... (w)hile a husband should
be at least twenty a girl should be married immediately
before puberty.

The Wonder That Was India by A. L. Basham

My grandmother was married off two days shy of her tenth birthday. My mother found a husband when she was twenty. I thus reckoned that if every generation increased by a decade the acceptable age for marriage, I should have become a wife by thirty.

But at thirty-three, I was nowhere close to being married. And it was this that brought much consternation to all, tainting the joy and inciting hitherto suppressed family politics, at the wedding of my twenty-two-year-old cousin, Nina.

I was at a family wedding in Bombay, the city where I was born and had spent most of my life. My parents and two brothers still lived here, in the same house that I knew as a child, a house conveniently located just minutes from major temples and hotels. Which was a good thing considering how much time they spent at such institutions, attending weddings just like this one. It was always, of course, someone else's wedding and never my own.

Nina had 'jumped the queue' as they all liked to say. She was much younger, and marrying before me. But then, as Nina's mother pointed out, how long could everyone wait?

I forced myself to smile and look happy. It wasn't that I was unhappy. It was just that, on this steaming May evening, I was hot and flustered, conscious of the damp fog-grey semi-circles formed by droplets of sweat on the underarms of my sari blouse. I had to press my limbs down against my body so they wouldn't show against the pale fabric. Both the sari and blouse were creamy whipped pink, like the pearly sheen of the inside of a seashell, or of little girls' bows. Six yards of the fabric were wrapped, nipped and tucked around my body, making me look – in my estimation – like a blushing eggroll. At least that was what I told anyone who complimented me.

I had been fidgeting all evening with the flowers in my hair. They were *faux*, bought off a wooden stand on a Bombay street-corner, papery and the size of a fingernail, about a dozen of them pinned into my upswept coiffure. Not exactly my idea of understated chic. But the hairdresser had insisted: 'Your cousin is getting married! You need some decoration!'

Thankfully understated wasn't the order of the day here

at the Jhule Lal Temple. Nina was about to become a wife in the presence of three hundred people, most of whom she had never met. I felt self-conscious standing there on the sidelines, the older, unmarried cousin, aware that people were glancing over at me – yes, to see what I was wearing, but mostly to detect any hint of pain or jealousy on my face as yet another younger cousin married. I closed my eyes for a second, inhaled, found my centre – the way they taught me to do at my Wednesday evening Hatha yoga class. Then, I lifted up my smile, and made it stay.

'Your turn next,' said Auntie Mona, my mother's second cousin, who was standing next to me. She grinned, revealing a space between her two front teeth the size of East Timor. That gap was considered a sign of good luck. Any Indian face-reader worth his *chapatti* dinner knew that the wider the space, the greater the fortune. 'Don't worry, *beti*, it will be your turn soon,' Auntie Mona consoled, patting me on the back. 'God will listen to your prayers. It's all karma. Tsk Tsk.'

I allowed her to comfort me, as I had learnt to do all these years, and noted how miraculous it was that my self-esteem wasn't completely annihilated by now. Since arriving in Bombay a week ago, I had been on the receiving end of many things: advice, sympathy, concern. But mostly, it was pity and consolation. Now, coming from Auntie Mona, these sentiments were delivered with the same gravity as a diagnosis of Lyme disease. My relatives never thought to ask about my interesting and independent life in New York, what I did there, who my friends were, or whether I'd scored a ticket to *The Producers* while Matthew Broderick and Nathan Lane were still in it. Instead, it was an incessant: 'Why aren't you married yet?'

I turned towards Nina, who really was the sweetest thing, looking a dream in her wedding sari. This was pink too, but a celebratory pink: deeper, richer, embellished with thick gold, a bridal bonus. The top of her gleaming black hair, parted down the centre, was covered with the same fabric, her smooth white forehead dotted with tiny flecks of red paint in an arched design spliced in the middle by a gold-and-diamond bindi. Her hands, lavishly hennaed, reached up to push back a wisp of hair that had fallen into her half-closed eyes. Nina was praying, and blushing, swooning from the heat. She and her groom were sitting in front of a small bright orange fire, both sets of parents by their side, deep in their own thoughts as our family priest, Maharaj Girdhar, uttered thousands of Sanskrit words that no one but him understood.

The ceremony was about done, and now came my favourite part – when the groom slipped his finger into a pot of *sindoor* – and traced it down his new wife's hair-parting. The gesture seemed to say, 'You're mine now. We belong to each other.' He looked at her with something that appeared to be pride mixed with awe. While it might not yet be love, the happiness seemed real, born of gratitude. He also seemed relieved. He had done it; he'd found the perfect bride and the fun could start. Later, they would spend their first night together, and kiss for the first time.

The groom had won Nina's heart without really trying. She'd fallen for his looks, his height (five feet eleven), his casual, easy-going demeanour. It was an arranged match. They had met twice, and then got engaged. That had been five weeks ago.

The couple stood, poised to garland one another and exchange rings. Nina bowed her head before her new husband, who looked upon her excitedly, like an archaeologist who had just stumbled across some rare artefact and couldn't wait to examine it. Within seconds, they were surrounded by waves of well-wishers who hugged, kissed, shook hands and leaned in to see up close just how big the necklace was that Nina's parents had given her. Everybody wanted to know the precise carat weight of the marquise diamond her groom had placed on the slender ring finger of her left hand.

It was time for me to make my way through the pack of people towards the couple. En masse, they smelt of sweat, turmeric, *paan* leaves and Pantene hair oil. I could detect here and there a whiff of Charlie perfume that I knew had been sitting in someone's metal Godrej cupboard for fifteen years. I winced for a second, but when I reached them, summoned up all my warmth and goodwill and embraced them.

'You look gorgeous, honey, I'm so happy for you. God bless,' I said, kissing Nina's smooth, warm cheek.

'*Didi* Anju,' she whispered, taking my hand. I loved how she always referred to me as *didi* – big sister. 'I said a prayer for you while I was walking around the fire taking my vows. You'll be next. I asked God, and God always listens to the prayers of brides.'

The pure sweetness of the gesture made me want to cry, but tears here would be misconstrued as a sign of longing and sadness, so I pinched them back. I turned to the groom, and looked up at him. 'Congratulations, sweetie,' I said, reaching up to hug him. 'You look after her.'

I became, as the word *didi* implied, the generous, solid, single, big sister.

That duty done, I turned and wove my way through the clusters of chattering people who were shuffling out of the hall to a large dining room below. I found my parents in one corner and padded, still barefoot, over to them. Next would come the horror of trying to find my shoes in the pile outside. Bombay weddings were notorious for shoe theft, and I began wondering – belatedly – how good an idea it had been to wear my Dolce & Gabbana mules today.

'OK, come, let's go downstairs and eat,' said my mother, as she automatically adjusted the part of my sari that was coming undone.

My father was mopping the sweat from his brow with a handkerchief.

'Too damn hot,' he said. 'Let's go downstairs. Maybe it's cooler there.'

The large air-conditioners rumbled away, blowing frosty air on the long lines of people forming at the buffet table. My father put away his handkerchief, and picked up a plate.

'OK,' said my mother, turning to me. 'Have you seen anyone here you like? Any nice boys?'

'Mum, I haven't really been paying attention,' I replied. 'I wanted to watch the wedding ceremony properly.'

Again, my mother sighed, and looked around. People carrying plates piled with spicy aubergine and vegetable biryani were starting to fill up the rows of plastic chairs that had been set out.

That's when she spotted him.

'Who's he?' my mother asked, a finger pointing at a stranger in black across the room. 'The boy talking to Maharaj Girdhar.'

'Mum, stop pointing! And how am I supposed to know?' I was getting testy. This was inevitable, this scouting around for available men at a family wedding. But I was hot and tired, my sari felt like it was coming unwrapped, and, a day away from getting my period, I just wasn't in the mood. My psychic, had he been there, would have said that I was experiencing a mild form of resentment at Nina's new matrimonial state, that it had brought up my worst fears about my own future. Because he had been right about such reactions in the past, I decided on the spot that from now on, I'd save the money I'd spent on him for shoes.

But the Great Official Husband-Hunt, as I had come to call it, was well under way. I had been here for several days, and there had been some talk of this boy and that. Tonight, my mother had spotted a real-life prospect.

I turned to look at the man, and I was struck by the extreme shininess of his hair, as if he had emptied an entire bottle of Vitalis oil on to it. He also had one eyebrow. Well, not strictly one eyebrow, but two that merged in the middle. I fought the urge to run home and find my Tweezerman. He wore a black shirt with little shiny translucent stripes running through it, a white short-sleeved undershirt and black trousers. And white socks. There was also a big gold pendant hanging from a chain around his neck, a shiny bracelet and diamond-studded watch. Looking at him, I felt like I was having an eighties moment.

'Wait a minute,' my mother instructed, and moved off to consult with Nina's new mother-in-law. I knew she figured that if the man she saw was not from our side of the family, then he must surely be from the other.

At that precise second, the guy with one eyebrow turned to look at me. My stomach sinking, I saw him lean over and say something to Maharaj Girdhar, who quickly moved to intercept my mother. The two talked quietly for a few minutes, while I stood alone, in my shimmering pinkness, looking around awkwardly. I knew I should be off celebrating and chatting inanely with random family members, but just couldn't summon up the initiative.

I saw my two younger brothers, surrounded by a gaggle of girlies who were brilliant and shiny in their embroidered saris, dangling earrings and colourful bangles. My brothers were the undisputed Princes William and Harry of this community, albeit somewhat older than the British royals. Anil was twenty-nine and Anand two years younger, and they were the hottest and most eligible boys around. In their Indian silk outfits, both clean-shaven, hair combed neatly back, their smiles revealing perfect teeth and an attitude often described in these parts as 'happy-go-lucky, easy-coming-easy-going', they looked as if they'd just stepped off the set of a Listermint commercial. Other, younger, girls on the Great Husband-Hunt were mesmerized by them – as were their pushy mothers. Of course, the fact that the boys stood, one day, to inherit a substantial jewellery and antiques business didn't hurt their combined appeal. I figured I would go and join them and let the young girls be fawningly nice to me. Always a plus to having an eligible brother or two.

But first I saw my father stepping outside alone, so I followed him.

He was looking over the metal gates surrounding the temple, and out on to the sea. He seemed wistful, perhaps remembering all the family weddings he had attended here, in this very temple – three in the past year alone – and how at each one he had prayed that the next time he came it would be to give his own daughter away.

He closed his eyes, took a deep breath. When he opened

13

them, he saw me walking towards him, negotiating my way on ridiculously high-heeled shoes that he knew I had spent way too much money on.

'Fresh air,' he said, enjoying a rare moment of calm in what had been a wedding-crazed week. 'All is well. God is great,' he sighed, pensive and calm.

I paused, then said, 'It stinks out here. Daddy, this is so *not* fresh air. You'd have a better chance of finding it standing on the corner of Madison Avenue and Fifty-Seventh. I can *see* your lungs blackening! Come on, let's go back in,' I said, hoping to interrupt his regretful thoughts about me, if that was indeed what preoccupied him.

Back in the temple hall, my mother, beaming, rejoined us.

'Anju, *beti*, he's asked for you. That boy. Maharaj Girdhar said he likes you and wants to meet you. What do you think?'

Part of me, I had to concede, was flattered. It was not every day that a man would look at me across a crowded, overheated room, and decide right off that he wanted to marry me. The last time it happened, I'd been with my girlfriends in a seedy salsa club on Eighth Avenue and Thirtieth Street. There, a man in a polyester pinstriped suit and a handlebar moustache told me he wanted to marry me, right before he threw up in a potted plant. That, pitifully, had been my last proposal.

And that was basically what this was. As loose an

14

expression of interest as it seemed, this was a proposal, no doubt about it.

There was, however, the whole issue of first impressions. The last man I'd dated wore Prada. No gold, no gum. He'd been cool. And he had neat eyebrows. But there certainly had been no proposal forthcoming.

But, here and now, my mother didn't want to hear about bad dress sense. That was an unacceptable reason to say no.

'What shall I tell Maharaj?' she asked me again.

'Mum,' I whispered, 'he looks like he should be on some America's Most Wanted list.'

'Anju, be serious!'

'OK, OK. Where's he from?'

'Accra.'

'As in Accra, Ghana, West Africa?' I exclaimed. 'What the hell am I going to do in Accra?'

'Don't say hell here, *beti*. People will hear you. They'll think you have no manners.'

Mr Monobrow was a vague distant relative of the groom, here to find a wife. He was from a well-to-do family that had made its money in grocery stores, my mother told me.

'*Beti*, Maharaj says he's a very *good* boy. Very good family. Plenty of money. At least meet him, no?'

'I'm sure he's perfectly nice, Mum, but really, I can't imagine living in Accra. I mean, aren't there military coups there every five minutes? And he just seems, you

15

know, a bit kind of uninteresting. I can't see that we'd have anything in common.'

My mother gave me that familiar look: the super-sized frustration-annoyance combo, with a side order of impatience thrown in.

'Anju, really, sometimes I think you have been in Umrica too long.' She sighed, and returned to the priest, who was waiting for an answer. She went to tell him they would think about it. In Indian-parent parlance, that meant she needed a day or two to convince me.

Mr Monobrow, in the meantime, had sidled off to the buffet table, with a short, plump woman who was probably his mother. I went off and found Namrata, Nina's eighteen-year-old sister, who had been given gift-holding duty.

'Hey, sweetie, what's up?' I asked.

'Nothing, *didi*. Just so tired. My feet are really paining me,' Namrata replied. She was toting a Singapore Duty Free Stores plastic bag filled with pretty envelopes, little silk purses and the odd velvet box, all containing cash, gold coins and jewellery.

'How are you, *didi*? Having a good time?' she asked.

Namrata was, like her sister, wholesome and good-natured. She reminded me of Britney Spears in her pre-sex siren days, all perky and popular, but minus the cropped tops and mini-skirts. Like her newly married sister, Namrata too could sing – from Hindi film songs to religious *bhajan*s. She had learnt how to pickle lemons

16

and fry *papad*s perfectly. And with her soft, fair, plump complexion, she was every Indian male's dream-wife. She looked a vision tonight, in a floaty lilac embroidered *gagara-choli*. She was being primed; her mother was already on the lookout for son-in-law number two. But Namrata was also bright and funny, not a cream-puff like so many of the other girls in this room, so I ran the Monobrow-dilemma by her.

'You see that guy over there?' I motioned to him. 'He told Maharaj Girdhar, who told Mummy, that he's interested in me. But he's from Accra. What am I going to do in Accra?'

Namrata glanced over at him, and a knowing smile spread across her pretty face.

'You know what it is, right, *didi*? In your baby-pink sari, you look like a marshmallow. All soft and sweet and fluffy and nothing inside but air. That's what *he* would want in a wife, don't you think?'

Two days later, I spent the morning with my mother at Bhuleshwar market. If there were such a thing as an urban purgatory, this would be it. Strings of small shops lined a road that wasn't quite a road. Cars were stalled every two feet by a dead cow, a sleeping homeless person or hawkers selling food. They heaved around worn wooden carts filled with plastic buckets and stainless steel forks, weaving their way in and out of the hundreds of people crammed throughout this smelly, fly-infested labyrinth.

We embarked from the quiet and cool sanity of our white Ambassador car and joined the approximately seventeen million other pedestrians. The only way to really 'do' Bhuleshwar was to walk it. The stench of cow dung in the heat was overwhelming; sweaty people pressed against me. Scrawny men with *paan*-stained teeth heckled and cat-called as we stopped intermittently at a stall here and there to shop. My mother chastised me for wearing embroidered capri pants and a slightly cropped white Martin Margiela T-shirt. 'You should have put on a cotton salwar kameez, *beti*. Now they all know you are a foreigner.'

The purchases, however, were worth the horrors. I bought thick copper bangles, packets of bindis and little painted clay dishes that Indian families use to hold devotional flames. I'd give those to my best friend Sheryl for her Tribeca loft where they would look great as trinket boxes. We selected a bale of woollen shawls, and countless yards of coloured silks that Marion, Erin, Kris and the other girls from work would fashion into cool cushion covers or summery sarong skirts. I found mirrored slippers that sold at Scoop for two hundred dollars ('What nonsense!' my mother screeched when I mentioned this), and which sold here for the equivalent of four dollars. See, there was much to return to Bombay for!

We were home in time for lunch, before the sun became too hatefully hot.

I grew up in this apartment on Warden Road, a nice residential part of the city not far from the sea. The cool of the marble in our entry corridor felt delicious against my bare feet. The apartment took up the whole of the top floor in a seven-storey building. It had once been two three-bedroomed suites but now had been combined into one rather oddly laid-out but grand six-bedroomed home. My grandfather had had the foresight to buy both units when he fled with his young family from Pakistan to Bombay around the time of the partition in 1947. He'd been able to sell his land in our family's original homeland of Hyderabad Sind, and came across the border on trains piled with other refugees, his pockets filled with old gold coins collected over the decades. With the help of relatives, he'd bought property, set up a jewellery business and raised his family safely away from the chaos over the border.

As we entered my mother reached out to touch the feet of a big stone statue of Lord Ganesh by the entrance, something she did each time she went out and returned home. I always resolved to emulate her, but mostly I forgot.

'I'd love some tea, Mummy,' I said as I dumped the flimsy shopping bags in my bedroom. I suddenly craved a steaming hot cup of the rich, cardamom-laden milky *chai* that Starbucks tries to do authentically.

'Chotu, *chai laikhe ao*,' my mother called out to the family cook, who was busy preparing dhal and *pulao* and *pakoda*s.

My father was sitting on the burgundy silk settee, reading *The Times of India*, his legs stretched out over a mirrored coffee table.

'Heat-wave in New York, it says here,' he announced, looking up. 'Why are you leaving so soon? I'm sure the airline can change your booking for tomorrow, maybe postpone it a few days,' he said.

'Dad, I need to get back to work, I only took two weeks off. The wedding is over, it was nice, time to go. Plus I'd rather suffer heat stroke in New York than hang around here. You know what I mean?'

I didn't want to hurt my parents. This was, after all, their home – as it once was mine. I didn't want to seem dismissive – as if I was now better than all this, as if I had left them behind for what I perceived to be a more worthwhile life. But as much as I wanted to please my parents, I couldn't stay here a day more than I had to.

I joined my father on the couch and turned to look outside the window. There was never anything other than complete pandemonium on the streets of Bombay. The cars seven floors below honked furiously, futilely, for no reason other than to hear the sound of their horns. Pedestrians darted in and out between vehicles and motor-cycles – called 'scooters' in these parts – with complete disregard for their lives. They had a fatalism about them:

get run over, lose a limb, all meant to be, whatever. Huge billboards painted with the faces of the hot stars of today, Hrithik Roshan and Karisma Kapoor, stood atop rickety buildings. In India, everything looked as if it were on the verge of collapse. I spotted another billboard across the street, advertising a new health club. 'Open from 5 in the morning until 11 in the night!' it trumpeted. 'Come on, get FIT and look COOL!' The visuals featured what appeared to be a couple of amputated pecs and a hacked-off torso. Fine art in the world of advertising was not a forte of my homeland. But still, this was the new Bombay, one in which women's magazines advertised condoms, sultry Bollywood love scenes were filmed, barely clothed MTV starlet-veejays and *Baywatch* bodies ruled the small screen and everyone was having affairs.

And marriages were still arranged.

A navy Mercedes pulled up on the street just outside the building, depositing three well-dressed, polished-looking women – Indian, but obviously not living in Bombay – on the pavement. They made their way into Benzer, a chic store across the way. They scowled at the broken paving stones, littered with cow dung and refuse. Bombay had evidently been their home once too, and now, like me, every time they came back, it became more and more a home they no longer recognized nor resonated with.

While lunch was being prepared, and I was enjoying my *chai*, my mother was on the phone with her sister Jyoti, Nina's mother. The newlyweds had gone off

21

honeymooning in southeast Asia, and then they would fly off to London, where they'd be living.

'Ay, Leela, I miss Nina,' Jyoti wailed. 'She's left the house, she's no longer my daughter, she belongs to someone else.'

'Ay, Jyoti,' my mother consoled her, as if someone had just died. 'It has to happen for all of us. The girls must get married and leave. Be grateful, your daughter has found a good boy, she'll be happy, don't worry. See, I'm still waiting for my Anju to find someone. No other boys came from overseas for the wedding?'

'What about the Accra fellow?' Jyoti asked. 'Maharaj Girdhar called today. He says the boy is very interested. I think you should pursue it.'

'Hah. Let us see. We'll talk about it over lunch.'

Chotu, our cook of twenty years, appeared from the kitchen carrying a large stainless steel tray bearing steaming, richly spiced dishes of food. A good Bombay meal was one of my favourite things about coming home. Hot, soft *pulao* embedded with *mung dahl*. Spinach smeared around chunks of *paneer*, soaked in a dozen freshly ground spices. Bite-sized *pakoda*s dipped in mint chutney and eaten with thick white bread. Ulrika, the goddess of New York fitness trainers, would positively pulverize me if she could see me now.

'*Beti*,' my mother said as she ladled out some food onto a plate for my father. 'The Accra boy is still here. Why don't you meet him?'

She paused, waiting for my response. I didn't provide one, so she asked again.

'So, what do you say?'

The guy hadn't even crossed my mind since the night of the wedding, I thought guiltily. I was poised to get on a plane the next day, to fly back to New York, my home for the past seven years, and to my job as a fashion publicist. Though I loved my job, and loved living in the city, it wasn't getting any easier for me there. So many men, but none of them quite what my parents had in mind for me. And because of some weird cultural osmosis that I had unwittingly succumbed to, I felt they weren't right for me either. I was on the party circuit, hung out at hip restaurants in the city, and because of my job, even went on the occasional junket to Europe. But most of the men I had met were gay, or white, and usually both.

My parents, perversely, thought gay was fine. When I was thirty, my mother had introduced me to a nice Indian boy from a nice Indian family. I had known right away; the red Versace leather trousers gave him away, as did his endearing – but ultimately condemning – interest in my Manolo Blahnik collection. After gay suitor and his mother had left, I voiced my reservations to my mother, who dismissed them with a simple: 'Once they marry, they change.'

'I doubt it, Mum,' I had said. 'Elton John: case in point.'

Pretty much once a year, every year since I had moved to New York, I'd been hauled back to Bombay for a look-see. All my cousins had done it that way, usually meeting their spouses at a family wedding. It was almost a domino-effect, although I thought it interesting that I was the only female cousin still left standing, with the exception of Namrata, and another, who was only eleven. Even she would probably find a husband before me at the rate all this was going. I had also been told that, at Nina's wedding, at least five girls had expressed their interest in 'either one' of my brothers. Such was the grab-bag nature of the game.

That I had received one expression of interest was in itself of tremendous significance. Bombay, after all, was a matrimonial melting-pot. All a single person need do is show up, make a few calls, pray, seek the advice of astrologers, family priests and professional matchmakers. And then pray some more that these people had some idea what they were doing. And most importantly, as my mother never failed to remind me, it was all about compromise.

From my family's perspective, this proposal was a big deal. Someone had literally 'asked for' me, and it was an honour, any way they looked at it. I had always told them I really *wanted* to get married. Truly I did. I wanted to slip back into the system. Yet I had been away so long now that often it was like I'd been for-gotten by the society I was born into. I realized that

24

when an attractive, eligible man appeared on the scene, I wouldn't be the first choice because I was living alone in New York, far removed from the matrimonial-minded masses.

I was oddly drawn to the age-old system of arranged marriage – it seemed exotic somehow, noble, and fragile. Observing the tradition would elevate me to the highest ranking on the scale of social conduct; when a girl marries a man her family members select for her it is the ultimate act of piety, and, according to tradition, would bring many, many blessings.

On each of my trips back to Bombay, I secretly hoped that this would be the special, destined journey in which I would find 'the one'. That here, in the midst of the wedding parties and politics and desperate mothers seeking boys and girls for their offspring, I, too, could find my intended.

On this trip, now, there was a proposal.

But, for God's sake, he lived in Accra.

'*Beti*, it's not the place, it's the person,' my mother said, reading my mind in that most inconvenient way that mothers do. 'If he's a good boy, then you'll be happy anywhere you go.'

Nice thought. But I still wasn't buying it.

'What do you think?' my mother asked my father.

After thirty-five years of marriage, my mother still never addressed her husband by his first name. She had told me when I was very young that wives should refer to their husbands only with a very grand 'he'. Anything else would be defamatory. 'Your husband will be your lord, and you must treat him with dignity and respect,' she had said. I must have been five.

But now, my father was stumped for an answer. He was no longer as involved with my matrimonial affairs as he had been, say, fifteen years ago. In fact, he would commonly say that he had 'given up', which hardly inspired hope and confidence in my beleaguered and perpetually single thirty-three-year-old heart.

At last, my father spoke. 'We should definitely consider it,' he said, wrapping a floppy brown piece of *chapatti* around a chunk of *paneer*. 'You're here, so you may as well get the job done. That way, at least your airfare won't be wasted.'

After lunch, my mother telephoned Maharaj Girdhar.

'Yes, I'm calling about the Accra boy,' she said, as if responding to an ad in the *Village Voice* about a second-hand Volkswagen. She grabbed a piece of paper and pen, and started scribbling.

'Yes ... of course ... good ... oh, almost thirty-nine? ... Very good ... Educated ... Well-to-do and all ... Good ... Yes, I'll talk to my husband and call you ... No, Anju is supposed to be leaving tomorrow, but of course if something works out, she'll stay. Her job in New York is not so important, hah? She must see the boy first, no?' she said in a conciliatory tone, wanting to please the priest as he, evidently, held the key to my future happiness.

She hung up, and turned back to us.

'OK, so here are the details. He's almost thirty-nine, which is a good age. Five foot eight, which is quite a good height, OK not so tall, but then you're not that tall and you'll maybe have to stop wearing such high high heels,' she said. Scanning her notes, she went on. 'Only son, one sister married, they have their own business, some shops, even a factory. Rich. Parents are nice. He also went to school in America. He travels here and there, I'm sure he'll take you along.'

She paused, having felt she'd done a sufficiently convincing sales pitch. 'He seems to have everything. What else do you want?' she asked, reasonably.

'Well, it's just that I have a nice life in New York,' I began. 'And I'm sure he's a decent enough fellow, but I don't think Accra is the place for me.'

'*Beti*, do you want to stay unmarried for ever?' my mother countered. 'Just imagine, if you met someone, and you married him, and he lived in a place you don't mind living in, such as New York or London or Singapore, and then something happened and he had to move to not such a nice place, like maybe even Accra. Are you saying that you wouldn't go with him? That is what marriage is, sacrifice and compromise.'

'Yes, I understand, Mummy, but I'm not married to

him so the sacrifice thing doesn't come up. I have the choice right now. You know what I'm saying?'

I looked at my mother's slowly greying hair, elegantly swept off her smooth and unlined face, the prize feature of which was her regal, haughty nose. She was wearing a polyester kaftan, similar to one of those 1970s-style Gucci djellabas from a few seasons ago, but this one had been made by the family tailor. It was my mother's preferred choice of stay-at-home clothing.

'Anju, you can't have everything in life. You can't be too hoity-toity. Didn't Maharaj tell you so many years ago that you have to learn to compromise? Where will you find everything you want in one boy? It's not possible, *beti*. You're already almost thirty-four. Soon, no one will ask for you any more. You must think carefully.'

I *was* thinking carefully. About waking up to Matt Lauer every morning, about the paraffin manicures and oxygen facials at Bliss, and Saturday afternoons shopping in Nolita. And the parties and fund-raisers. And waiting to see if Paris Hilton and Aerin Lauder would turn up, and what the fabulous ex-Miller girls would wear. And trying every different flavour of Martini, every new designer shoe, and giggling with my girlfriends as I listened to the stories of the boys in their lives. It had taken me some years, but now it was a life I had grown intimately familiar with and happily accustomed to. And, like so many women in my situation, I wanted a man to fit in neatly with it. I wanted him to live the same life, enjoy the same things, look the part. And, simultaneously, I wanted him to be chosen by my parents, sanctioned by the rest of the family. It wasn't much to ask for, was it?

But I also knew that in the view of my society, a woman was never much of anything until the day she got married. She was always a guest in her parents' home, they were her temporary caretakers. When the right man came, regardless of where or how he lived, this young, single woman would wrap her life around his. It was not about what she wanted, it was about what *he* wanted for both of them. Given that view, I remembered how my mother was baffled one time, watching an American TV movie, where a woman left her perfectly nice husband because she said she wanted to 'find herself'.

'Such nonsense,' Mummy had said. 'He's not beating her, he's not doing anything wrong. She wants to leave, for what? Stupid woman.'

My mother just didn't get it, but there was no reason she should. Her life had been all about sacrifice and compromise, the same virtues she plugged to me every day. My parents met once, and were engaged within five hours, married after two weeks. Together, they created a life that they had helped ease one another into. But they were both twenty when they met, and the word 'option' didn't exist for them. As my mother never failed to remind me, by the time she was my current age, she had been married thirteen years and had had all three of her children.

Yes, I deeply wanted to get married. I associated it with love and commitment and security – plus all the parties and new saris and a trousseau full of pretty dresses. But a family wedding in Bombay was one thing; a lifetime in Accra something else entirely.

'Mummy, I decided a long time ago that it was going to be G Eight only. You know, developed nations or nothing. Plus, there is the issue of compatibility here. We don't *look* compatible.'

My father interjected.

'What? Is he too short for you?'

'*No!*' I said emphatically. 'Look, there's got to be a vibe that happens between two people; you know, kind of a connection. You just get it – either it's there, or it's not.'

'*Aarey*, I don't know what you're saying,' my mother replied.

'I just want to be happy, Mummy.'

'*Beti,*' she replied, 'I don't want you to be happy. I want you to be married.'

Chapter Two

It is considered highly improper for a young man or woman to take the initiative for his or her marriage. With the spread of education nowadays the boy and the girl are given a chance to see each other unlike the old days when the newlyweds saw each other after the marriage.

Hinduism: an Introduction by Dharam Vir Singh

There seemed to be nothing more for it but to call Delta Airlines and change my flight. My mother had implored me to stay in Bombay just a few more days, convincing me that since the wedding had only just finished, calls would be made and somehow between all my family members we could find out if there were any interesting, suitable boys floating around. Of course, my mother then had to casually suggest it: '*Beti*, while you are still here, why don't you meet the boy from Accra? You can't just look at how he was dressed, a wife can always change her husband's clothes,' she had reasoned. 'And so? What's wrong with white socks?'

Maharaj Girdhar worked quickly and set up a meeting for the following evening at the Sea Lounge in the Taj Mahal Hotel. He wasn't going to waste any time. If this thing went through, he would collect twenty-five thousand rupees as a matchmaker's fee – about the price of a small Louis Vuitton handbag – certainly more than enough for him to live on for the next six months. He had organized Nina's match, so he felt he was on a roll as far as my family was concerned. Unlike with dating agencies, there was no payoff for him until the deed was done; he wouldn't collect a paisa for simply setting up a meeting. This was an interesting metaphor for the Indian-style matrimonial game. The jackpot is a wedding, and there are no consolation prizes. It's all or nothing.

The Accra boy project had begun to acquire a momentum all its own, and it had swept me away. No matter how hard I looked, there simply was no good enough reason to say no – the whole 'I don't like the way he looks' excuse just didn't fly any more. On the instruction of my parents, I had emailed my boss, Marion, and told her I had caught a touch of dysentery, and the doctor thought I shouldn't travel. Marion emailed back, and said fine, absolutely, we've got everything under control. Evidently she was aware I was fibbing too, because she added a PS: 'Have you found a husband yet?'

At six the following evening, my parents and Anil – the older of my two brothers – walked ahead of me as we all trod up the wide, red-carpeted staircase leading from the lobby of the Taj to the Sea Lounge. This was one of my favourite haunts in Bombay: a couple of times in the past week, while the rest of the family had been busy with wedding preparations, I had escaped here with a copy of the latest *Vanity Fair*, and sat and sipped fresh

34

young coconut water while occasionally looking through the open windows on to the Gateway of India and the sea beyond. Neutral ground, light and breezy: it was not surprising that the place was a popular venue for fix-ups of this nature.

Aunt Jyoti had wanted me to go ethnic, in just a simple salwar kameez. 'It's better, Anju, you'll look more Indian, more *domesticated*.'

But I had said that I would feel much more comfortable, and therefore exude a more relaxed air, if I slipped into a silky BCBG dress. It was sufficiently modest not to offend any sensibilities, yet feminine enough so that, when I was fully dressed, my mother had glowed at me in delight. She wanted me to wear some nice jewellery – enough to show the Accra family that we were people of means, yet not so much that the man in question would think that I was some high-maintenance diva-de-luxe. It was a delicate balance.

They were already there, seated at a corner table, with Maharaj Girdhar. The spacious, comfortable lounge – all cosy aqua-green chairs and natural lighting – was filled with the genial buzz of conversation.

The name of the intended was Puran. Next to him was his mother, the woman I had seen him with at the buffet table at Nina's wedding. With them was also a sad-looking man – the father, I figured. Puran was still chewing gum, and I fervently hoped it wasn't the same stick from the other night. I tried not to stare at his one eyebrow, bushy and unkempt, reminding me of two baby ferrets lying nose-to-nose. But there was something else . . . he was wearing the same semi-transparent black shirt and the same black trousers that he had worn at the wedding. As I walked closer, I noticed that his trousers had little flowers embossed up and down the leg. Someone, I thought, should get this man a stylist.

They stood as we approached, and awkward hand-shakes and introductions were exchanged all round while I smiled nervously, wanting to be pleasant and affable and enter into the spirit of this thing, yet utterly convinced in my soul that this was never going to happen.

'Anju, why don't you sit there,' my mother entreated, pointing to an empty seat on the other side of the prospective groom. Good thing I was wearing my slides, as Puran appeared shorter than I remembered him. Drinks were ordered, small-talk made ('So hot here these days, Bombay is getting worse and worse,' announced Puran's father), and both mothers complimented one another on their saris. I said nothing. I had been through so many of these that by now I knew the drill intimately. It went something like this:

1. Wait until the boy speaks first.

2. Smile.

3. Reveal as little as possible. (In the words of my mother's guru from years ago: 'Don't show you have any opinions or intelligence. Boys don't like it. You can say what you want after you're married, but until then,

be quiet.' It was straight out of *The Rules*. And it hadn't worked thus far.)

'So, you like Bombay?' Puran's mother asked me.

I smiled and nodded

'You must be liking New York also?' the father asked. 'What is your work there?'

'I, um, just work in an office, they do like, um, an advertising type of business,' I replied, knowing I should dumb-down my life. Puran still hadn't uttered a word to me or to anyone else at the table, immersed as he was in the task of stirring his mango juice with a plastic straw. I had opted for a *lassi*, but, at that moment, would have sacrificed a Fendi bag for a Cosmopolitan. I smirked at the thought of how ordering a vodka-heavy drink would look to my potential in-laws.

'So, Puran,' my father began, taking on the tone of a paternal job interviewer. 'I understand you have some shops in Accra?'

Puran finally spoke, in a voice that sounded a bit more helium-enriched than I had imagined. 'Yes. Groceries, general provisions, like that,' he said, with no further elaboration.

'And how's business these days?'

'Up and down. There were some riots last year, and our stores were looted.'

I was not encouraged. Talk of anarchy on one's home front did not make for good first-date conversation. I glanced over at my brother for a show of support; Anil winked and smiled. 'Just pretend it's a game,' he seemed to be saying to me. An uncomfortable silence descended upon the table, as Puran's mother eyed me up and down, ascertaining if I was a daughter-in-law in the making.

No doubt, if this had been thirty years ago, my appearance would have been different. My mother went to meet my father for the first time wrapped in a blue silk sari, with jasmine flowers laced through her long, braided hair. She never looked up once. And the words 'New York' certainly never featured in the conversation. My father says he wanted to marry her as soon as he saw her enter the room. It was, actually, deeply romantic.

Most mothers of supposedly eligible Indian men want their sons to marry unspoiled and domesticated girls from wealthy families. That way, dowries are munificent yet the girl herself is acquiescent and non-demanding. It is the ideal. Puran's mother was no exception. She was clearly disapproving of the living-in-America factor, but was willing to overlook it when she thought of the kind of parties my family would throw to celebrate finally off-loading me. And the images of suitcases containing silver and silks, of the red velvet boxes carrying jewellery and gold coins that would be sent over to her in the run-up to the wedding ... well, what was a little independent streak in a daughter-in-law – one that could surely be quelled with marriage – in comparison to that?

'Puran, why don't you take Anju for a walk?' his mother suggested, smoothly segueing into the next step in the proceedings. Please say no, I silently beseeched. That would signal that he wasn't interested, that he had decided that I didn't suit him, and I could go home with my family, then fly back to New York, and never have to think of Accra again.

But Puran obediently put down his glass of mango juice, and stood up, turning to me and expecting me to do likewise. I had no choice but to rise; to refuse would have been hugely embarrassing for my parents, and I would never hear the end of it. I consoled myself with the fact that it was going to be a quick stroll around the interior of the hotel, no big deal, I could do this. Quickly, I reminded myself of all the things I should not say: my mother had fudged my age a bit, so I was really now only thirty. And not a word about the travel that had been integral to my job publicizing fashion designers – boys didn't want to hear about their prospective brides organizing back-stage interviews for Michael Kors in Paris. Say nothing unless asked, and if forced to speak of it, play it down. Doing otherwise would sabotage this from the outset, and my parents would have another 'rejection' on their hands. And my pride wouldn't allow me to be turned down by someone I would never marry. Ever. Even under the most dire and desperate circumstances.

'What time do you wake up in the morning?' he asked as we made our way across the lounge and through the double doors leading to the corridor outside.

'Excuse me?'

'What time do you wake up in the morning?'

'Um, well, here, because I'm on holiday, quite late, perhaps around ten or so, you know how it is when there's a family wedding and you're out every night. But in New York, generally, never later than seven. I try and get to the gym before I head off to work and . . .'

I realized I had revealed too much about my life already, and stopped. I mustn't sound ambitious or successful, so I just kept visualizing the word my young cousin Namrata had used: marshmallow. I was going to be a marshmallow, just for tonight.

'Because at home in Accra, everyone gets up early,' he countered. 'There is too much to do. So it's good you are an early riser. Easier for you to adjust.'

Much energy was now being spent on squashing the words inside me that were fighting to be spat out. The poor sod thought it was a done deal. In his mind, I was his wife already.

'We have three maids at home, and a cook, but they have to be supervised. It's a job for the woman of the house. All the work starts early in the morning. They still don't know how to use the vacuum cleaner. Do you know how to use a vacuum cleaner?'

I sighed. This is what my life had become. I was in one of the most beautiful hotels in Bombay, on a sultry evening, dressed in silk, sweet and smiling and basically being a delightfully charming dream-date. And walking next to me was a man who only wanted to marry me because he needed to supplement his domestic task force.

'My mummy tells me your work in Umrica is to do with fashion,' he continued. 'Do you like my trousers?' He stopped, lifted up one leg like he was a pooch about to pee, and pointed out the little embossed flowers. 'They are the latest thing,' he said proudly.

At some point, I phased out of the conversation, I'll admit.

'. . . and then on Sundays I take my mother to the market . . . we have three maids and a cook, but they have to be supervised, so it's better we do the vegetable shopping ourselves . . . you can't trust the natives, you give them money to buy aubergine, and they buy cigarettes instead and then say the money was stolen. Ridiculous! My mother sometimes doesn't feel like going to the market, you know, she's getting a little old now, so of course that will be a job for you. Then, every four Mondays, there's a picnic with all their friends, and I take them there. Do you like picnics? But sometimes it's too hot so we have to hold it in somebody's house. We play bingo. Do you play bingo?'

'When I'm not at a Tae-bo class, sure,' I replied. Puran just looked puzzled, and continued nattering on about his life in Accra – how he came home for lunch, but on the days he didn't, a 'tiffin' had to be sent to him at his office. His father was more or less retired now, so he had to run the business by himself, and it could be stressful, so it was time he found a wife. He needed someone he could come home to and who would pour him a whisky soda – although she wasn't allowed to drink with him, because he thought it was very bad for a woman to consume alcohol.

'And I like getting massage, do you know how to give massage?'

And on and on he went, not once asking me what I saw for my own life. Even if he had, I still wouldn't have wanted to marry him, but at least he wouldn't have come across as so ridiculously archaic. I didn't expect him to peer into my soul, but a smidgen of polite interest would have been nice. At least I hadn't deluded myself, as I had done so many times before, into thinking this could be Mr Right. If nothing else, this was just another story to regale the girls with when I finally got home. And they thought *they* had had bad dates.

'We'd better go back now, no?' I said to him, as we made our fifteenth circuit around the Taj lobby. He looked happy and satisfied, that perhaps after years of interviewing, he might just have found the right candidate.

'*Oh my God!*' I said to my parents, as soon as we were safely back in our car. 'What was that? *Who* was that? What were you thinking?'

'So that means you didn't like him, Anju?' my mother asked, innocently.

'*Like* him? *Like* him? What was there to like?'

'He didn't seem *that* bad,' said my father. 'And they're interested.'

Anil, who was sitting in the front passenger seat grinning, finally spoke.

'Yeah, they were already talking wedding dates while you guys went off for your romantic stroll,' he said. 'They want to do it before they fly back to Accra, so I guess in the next couple of weeks. You'd better start getting your stuff together, *didi*, you're going to be married!' he said.

'*Mum!*' I pleaded. '*Come on!*'

'If you're not interested, you're not interested,' she said, resignedly. 'I'll just tell them when they phone tomorrow. Of course, they'll tell Maharaj Girdhar that you're fussy, and then he won't call us if there are other boys, because he'll think you've become too hoity-toity, but what can we do? You're saying no, we have to say no.'

'Yes but, Mum, you know me. Did you honestly think that I'd be into someone like that. Honestly?'

'But, *beti*, look at your *age*! You're not twenty-two any more. You're not going to get proposals like Nina and Namrata. There aren't so many boys still unmarried who are older than you. Maybe he's not perfect, but at least he's like you. *Elderly-type*.'

As we all anticipated, the call came the next day. Maharaj Girdhar phoned to inform us that 'the boy's side says yes'.

It was a triumphant pronouncement – he had already no doubt decided on how he would spend his finder's fee. But more than that, he thought himself brilliant and clever for at last having found someone for me, that wayward girl who had left her family in Bombay and gone to live in Umrica, all alone. This would no doubt elevate his status within the religious-social circles in which he slithered.

It fell upon my mother to tell him otherwise. 'Sorry, Maharaj, but he's not for us,' she said quietly.

'But why?' the priest retaliated, sounding horrified, as if I had just turned down the hand of George Clooney. 'The boy is so good, everything is so good. So many girls were interested in him. See, they chose your daughter! How can you say no?'

'Sorry, Mum,' I said after she had put the phone down. 'But you know it would never have worked.'

'Really Anju,' she sighed, 'I don't know what you're looking for.'

Later that afternoon, Aunt Jyoti sent over a jar of cream. Someone at the wedding had pointed out that I 'had nice features, but was a little on the dark side'. Being fair-skinned was as important a criterion as having all one's limbs intact. Ordinarily, my complexion could be described as 'milky *chai*'. But perhaps I hadn't been using my sunscreen very faithfully: I had to concede it was now more like a double espresso. Fairness indicated fragility, docility, prettiness. A girl could be cock-eyed, buck-toothed and have had a botched rhinoplasty, but if she were fair, she was considered a beauty in the league of Catherine Zeta-Jones.

So I sat on my bed, holding a jumbo-sized tube of 'Promise of Fairness'. There were no ingredients listed on the container, but I had read somewhere about how the product was found to contain a high concentration of mercury. I called my aunt to inform her of this, and to tell her that if I used it, I would probably contract some ghastly skin disease like melanoma.

Aunt Jyoti quickly agreed. 'Yes, better not,' she said. 'If something goes wrong with your face, who will marry you?'

A slight depression fell over me as evening descended. It was another scorching night, and I was lying on my bed listening to vintage Toni Braxton on my CD player. I felt an odd *mélange* of melancholy and confusion. No return date finalized for New York, and not a lot to do here in the aftermath of the chaos of Nina's wedding. It was just a lot of waiting around, hoping – or at least my mother was – that the phone would ring with another offer.

So I hopped across the street to the neighbourhood internet café – in reality a bunch of computers and a coffee-maker stuck into an old garage. I passed a trio of fifteen-year-old boys downloading porn, and settled in front of an Acer to check my emails. There were thirty-five messages, mostly from my friends in New

45

York who were filling me in on *their* holiday plans. Sheryl was going down the Amazon. Marion was thinking the Pyramids. Erin was going to stay close, in the Hamptons.

'But you, sweetie, are having the most unique experience of all!' Sheryl wrote. ' A literal, far-reaching, no-stones-unturned quest for a husband! *So* brave! *So* Indiana Jones!'

At home an hour later, the phone rang. It was Rita Mehta, a professional matchmaker whom my mother had called a few days earlier. I listened as my 'details' were divulged: age – 'twenty-nine', a further reduction; height (five feet four), build (average), complexion (medium). So far, I hardly sounded scintillating or vibrant. No talk was made of preferences, hobbies, interests. Just how old, how tall, how slim, how fair.

'Is she very Umrican-type?' the matchmaker asked, when my mother reluctantly let on that I had been 'working in New York, temporarily, in an office'. 'I mean to say, can she adjust?' Rita clarified.

'She's a very *good* girl,' my mother said. 'Smart, but homely-type.' By that, my mother was wanting to drive home the point that I was a stay-at-home kind of girl, the gentle and subservient sort who would subjugate her own needs for the sake of a peaceful household. My mother wasn't far wrong, either. I was fairly sure my club-hopping, plane-changing days would stop the day I found a groom.

'She's living for a short while in Umrica now, but she's Indian at heart,' she continued, aware that my 'living in Umrica' thing was not just a fall from grace, it was a huge, almighty thud. Men who came to India to find wives generally didn't want women who had carved out independent lives for themselves away from their families. Mr Accra had chosen to ignore all that because it didn't seem too important, in the scheme of things. What he had wanted was someone who would marry him, move to his country, and above all spend the rest of her days memorizing the vacuum cleaner manual.

'We're looking for a good boy,' my mother continued. 'No bad habits.' That was an oblique reference to cigarettes, over-indulgence in alcohol, extravagant spending and womanizing – a proviso that basically eliminated everyone in my New York circle of friends.

She started scribbling some notes down again, in a small red notebook that had 'Boys' marked on the front. Sitting next to her, I saw her write 'Dubai, 36, own clothing shops, well educated', Lalit-something-or-another. A father's name, a mother's name.

Rita said: 'He's a very good boy, I've checked everything thoroughly. The boy is not in Bombay now, but if there is someone interesting, he'll fly down.'

This time, my mother didn't even consult me. Within

an hour, she was on the phone with a friend who had lived in Dubai.

'Can you make some inquiries, find out if the boy is good? It's for matrimonial purposes,' she asserted.

Poor fellow, I thought. He's probably out having a perfectly nice day, doing whatever they do for fun in the United Arab Emirates. Little did he know that before the end of the day, my family would know enough about him to do a Kitty Kelley.

As it turned out, Lalit had spent six months in jail for forging cheques. My father curtly said, 'Drop it. We don't want a criminal son-in-law.' But my mother thought he was acting too rashly.

'So? It's not like he murdered anyone. Plus, after marriage, he'll change.'

Another week passed. Sunday morning, and I joined my parents in leafing through *The Times of India* matrimonial pages. My father circled a couple of interesting prospects: 'Overseas Indian (Sindhi) male in mid-thirties seeking overseas Indian female of same caste. Must be at least 5'3", slim, medium complexion, good nature.'

My mother called the number on the bottom of the ad. 'Er, yes, hello, I'm calling about the boy in today's paper.'

A fleeting pang of guilt struck me. Going on thirty-four, I couldn't even find a mate on my own, and my mother was spending her Sunday mornings in the twilight of her life on the phone with the families of strange men.

'Yes, the girl is now here . . . We're local people, but she's living temporarily in New York, working in an office there . . . Yes, she's the right height . . . How old is the boy? . . . Hah, thirty-five, very good. And where does the boy live?' And so continued a barrage of questions to the woman on the other end, the sister of the boy in question.

'Hah, OK, yes,' she said, starting to scribble. Suddenly, she stopped writing, and quickly said: 'Hah, OK, OK, thank you, I'll talk to my daughter and phone you back,' before hanging up.

'So?' my father asked, looking up from the paper.

'He lives in Indonesia,' my mother said. 'He owns a small videotape copying shop, you know, people bring in their tapes and he has a lot of VCRs and he copies them.' She looked over at me. 'I didn't think you'd be interested.'

But then came something far more promising. A prospect from Spain. Madrid actually. Mmm, I thought. Romantic and cosmopolitan. The home of Loewe, and the Guggenheim Museum, Bilbao, and a stately King and Queen, and tapas and sangria. And at least a place where an electricity generator was not a mandatory household appliance.

He was a banker, thirty-seven, educated, good-natured,

tall, according to the ad. 'In Bombay from June 2 to 15.'

'That's now,' my mother announced, enthusiastically. She got on the phone again, this time reaching a very pleasant-sounding woman, who was apparently the prospect's mother. He went to Yale, and was head-hunted for a position starting up a new American bank in Spain. He had a sister at university in California, so apparently they were fairly liberal people. He had taken a few weeks off from work to be in Bombay, like myself, for matrimonial purposes. It was decided that, before it went any further, photographs should be exchanged. 'Quickly, go find one, something that doesn't make you look so old,' my mother instructed.

I may as well have been hunched over, clasping a cane, shuffling off into the next room. For an Indian woman, I was not just spinsterly; I was positively old-maidish. Knowing this made me laugh – but only because I'd cried enough about it in the past.

Marrying me off now, at this appallingly late stage, would require a miracle.

And some savvy marketing.

And a flattering photograph.

A couple of hours later, a driver appeared to deliver an envelope containing a photograph of the banker from Spain, and to pick up mine. I tentatively pulled out the colour print. It was a picture of him taken in an outdoor café: 'Barcelona, July 2000' was inked across the back.

He was wearing a Ralph Lauren polo shirt tucked into blue denim jeans. He was smiling, one finger resting lightly on the edge of an espresso cup, the sun shining down onto his black hair, a light shadow falling over part of his face. A good face it was, too. Open, kind, intelligent. He seemed nice, somehow, not like the sort of narrow-minded chumps who were on the prowl for another maid, another mother.

'You like him, no?' my mother asked when she saw a satisfied smile appear on my face.

'Well, he looks like a nice guy, Mum.'

It had suddenly become a situation full of possibilities. The possibility that my father would finally stop moaning about how I kept 'wasting airfare', that my mother's friends would stop 'tut-tutting' their way through their card-playing sessions about poor, perennially unmarried me. And, most importantly, the possibility that I could find someone for me, even if I wasn't the ideal Indian woman – someone with the talents of Martha Stewart and the body of Claudia Schiffer, a vegetarian teetotaller who never stopped smiling, praying, pleasing and nodding. That despite all this, maybe, just maybe, there was someone who wanted me anyway. As my more supportive relatives would always say: '*Beti*, the boy destined for you is already born. He is somewhere in the world. We just have to find him.'

The sun set, and a light breeze came in through the open windows. My father was asleep in his armchair, my mother went off to nap in the bedroom, and the boys were out somewhere. I was eating *dokhla*s – spongy semolina snacks served with a cool mint chutney, and watching rehashed coverage of the Tommy Hilfiger fashion show on CNN. I remembered being there, standing way at the back as all publicists do, ensuring that the *Vogue*s and *Elle*s and *In-Style*s were all happily seated. All the front row divas looked bored and constipated, as if they were doing the world a huge honour by simply showing up. All praying that they would be the ones seated next to the celebrity-of-choice at this particular catwalk show, maybe bold and brassy Samuel Jackson, or skinny, pretty, sad-looking Gwyneth Paltrow.

That had been my life – catwalks and cocktail parties and being able to say that I had been in the same room as Angelina Jolie. It was fun and frivolous, but that was it. The other day, I had read some of the pages in my journal from last year: 'Yes! Got the last Kate Spade bag in the Barneys sale!' or 'Why did I spend $1,500 at Patagonia when I hate hiking?' or 'Exhausted from power yoga, and not helped by the three Raspberry Stolis I had afterwards.'

There were no words about being moved in deeper ways, except for those occasions when I might have attended a meditation class and returned home vowing to change my life, become connected with the greater universe, find inner peace. But then *The West Wing* came on, and all was forgotten. Mine had become a life lived on the outside. And if I tried to probe to see what was beneath it, there would only be concealed neuroses and petty jealousies and more dysfunction than I could deal with. So instead, I'd have a Cosmopolitan, buy a pair of shoes, whatever. It was, essentially, a biodegradable life, one that, if I let it slip from my grip, would merge with the dirt and disappear, leaving nothing behind.

I needed a change. And perhaps that change could begin with marriage.

I said a silent prayer that the nice-looking man from Madrid would call. I hadn't even heard his voice, nor did I know anything about him beyond the basics. But he seemed closer to 'the one' than anyone I had come across in a long time. Like the struggling ingénue who has already written an Oscar-acceptance speech, I had yet to meet this man, but I had already named the children.

My parents finally stirred awake from their afternoon nap. 'Did they call?' my mother asked me. I shook my head. They all knew that for every hour that passed, it would be less and less likely that the phone would ring. I then realized that although I had liked the look of him, perhaps he didn't like the look of me. Could that be? I had sent along my most appealing photograph, taken in Central Park on a sunny afternoon, me in a summery pink top and white pants, subtly conveying some of that fluffy-marshmallow element, just in case. In the picture, my black hair, lightly tinted, looked shiny and lush under the sun, my smiling face a vision of relaxed happiness.

And I didn't look too dark-skinned either. How could anyone not like the look of me in that photograph?

I attempted to busy myself with various things, but every time the phone jingled, I stopped what I was doing and I prayed that this would be the call.

It never came.

Late the next afternoon, Aunt Jyoti stopped by for tea, and settled onto the sofa in preparation for a no-holds-barred gossip session that would last at least three hours.

'I hear the parents of that Madrid boy have been making inquiries about you,' she said to me, with the air of someone who had obtained classified information from the Pentagon.

'Oh, yes, we spoke to them yesterday,' my mother interjected, surprised. She had wanted to keep this quiet until something 'worked out', so ashamed had she become of the litany of failed alliances that trailed behind me. But Bombay was a small town when it came to things of a matrimonial nature, and it never took more than about four minutes for news of pitches and proposals to spread. I began to feel like one of those screenplays that get touted around Hollywood agents and studios and producers; everyone takes a quick look and passes, yet they continue knocking about ad infinitum.

'We exchanged pictures,' my mother said, figuring she may as well tell her sister all. 'We liked his. We didn't hear back. Maybe they didn't like how Anju looked. Oh well, can't be helped – these things happen.' For my sake, my mother forced a couldn't-care-less attitude, although I knew she was deeply disappointed. At last, she had come across someone her daughter seemed interested in, and this time *they* weren't interested. Karma, she thought. That's what everything comes down to.

'It's not her looks,' Aunt Jyoti said. 'The family made inquiries and heard that she has been living alone in New York for some time, that she was independent-type. The boy says girls like that can't be moulded. He wanted someone a bit more traditional-type. What can you do? You have to live with it.' My mother and aunt looked over at me with pity and tendernesss, as if I were a quadriplegic.

'That is *so* not on!' I cried out. 'I mean, this guy went away to university in the States, right? His sister is there, right? So what's the hypocrisy all about?'

'Anju, *beti*,' Aunt Jyoti started. 'It's not that. Boys feel it's OK for them, maybe even their sisters, but in the end, they don't want to marry a girl like that. He just doesn't like it that you have been living alone there, without your parents, for so many years. He feels that by now you will surely have become too much independent. I told you years back when you were going that this would happen. Now see? That's why I would never let my daughters go off like that,' she said, casting a look of disapproval at both my mother and myself, and recalling proudly how one daughter was snapped up at twenty-two, and surely the younger one would not be far behind.

My mother, surprisingly, stood up for me.

'Jyoti, boys should be more open-minded these days, more forward-thinking. If he doesn't want my daughter, that's his loss. We'll find someone better. He can just go marry some dumbo who can't even open her mouth without asking for permission.'

'You go, Mum,' I chimed in, smiling. I felt better now, knowing that my mother didn't chastise me – not in public, at least. At that moment, the phone rang. It was Sheryl, calling from New York.

'How's it all going over there? Married yet? Should I be booking airline tickets, buying the dress? Will you seat me next to someone cute?' she asked. She always spoke this way, always sounding breathless, rushed and enthused.

'Some guy from Spain who seemed interesting turned out to be a flake because he thought I was too independent. Me! I can't even find a man without my parents helping me. How independent is that?'

'Look,' said Sheryl. 'He probably just wants some submissive twelve-year-old. It's his prerogative, you know. It's like he went into Henri Bendel, saw a nice sweater, but it's been there for a while, marked down, on sale. So maybe he takes a look at it, puts it down, moves on to something else. Something in the new arrivals section. It's nothing personal. He just doesn't want that particular sweater.'

I could always trust Sheryl to reduce everything to a shopping expedition.

'Anyway,' she continued, 'you think you've got problems. I had a blind date last night, a fellow called Jerome my cousin set me up with. The date was fine, but when he dropped me home, he wanted to come up and use the toilet. After he left, I went in there and he had peed all over the place, on the floor, splashed around the toilet bowl. What do you think is the likelihood of me wanting to go out with someone who can't even pee straight?'

'I don't know, Sheryl,' I said. 'But I still think my dilemma is far worse than yours. I was rejected by a man before he even met me. Beat that.'

Chapter Three

The scriptures forbid the sacrifice of female animals, but in the case of human beings, sacrificing females gives the greatest satisfaction.

Chaturanga by Rabindranath Tagore

'I'm not understanding it,' my father said, putting down his newspaper and turning to look at my mother. 'There's nothing wrong with Anju. She's a pleasant enough girl, quite attractive. I'm not understanding how she's so unable to find a good boy.'

My mother turned her attention away from the Hindi comedy show – a rip-off of *The Brady Bunch* – that she was watching on Zee TV.

'It's God's way. We have done our best, and all now is in God's hand.'

I was in my bedroom, half reading an old Wodehouse book I had found lying around, in a failed bid to distract myself. All day long, I had only been able to think of my life in New York. The free concerts in Central Park would be starting soon, and the men's shows for fashion week would be under way in a few weeks. I had called Marion this morning and asked for an indefinite leave of absence.

Professionally, it was the most illogical thing to do. But I really did feel as if I had little choice if I was going to see this thing through.

'I need to show my parents that I'm making an effort,' I had told my boss. Yes, I was tearful, anxious, bored, desperate – a lethal combination sure to drive all the boys away. And yes, I wanted to return to my little apartment on the Upper West Side, to my girlie dinners alfresco, to finding clever ways to describe a new handbag collection in a press release, to my *Sex and the City* existence – minus the sex.

I loved my life there.

But I loved my parents more.

'Look, Marion, I don't know how long it's going to take, but I think I need to give it a fair shot. I had no idea when I left New York to come here for my cousin's wedding that I'd end up staying longer than two weeks, but that's what's happened, so I have to deal with it.'

'Are you sure you're OK with what you're doing?' Marion asked, a concerned tone in her voice. Fortunately for me, my boss was a sympathetic sort, and the complete antithesis of a fashion doyenne. She was a former rebirther turned PR guru who spent most of her time counselling the six neurotic female publicists and one hyper-neurotic gay male one she employed. She served us camomile tea and vegan cookies when we were having a bad day, hair-related or otherwise.

'Marion, I really appreciate you being this understanding.

Not a lot of bosses would let their staff have some time off to find a husband.'

She laughed. 'Honey, I'm not that altruistic. I'm just dying to come to an Indian wedding. So hurry up and get on with it. And by the way, I'm not that great a boss. I'm giving you leave, all right, but it's unpaid – we're not exactly Fortune Five Hundred.'

In August, I was turning thirty-four. As far as my community was concerned, I was already a write-off. As far as everyone else saw it, I was *always* going to be there, still single. There were some girls that all the boys wanted to marry, but I, sadly, wasn't one of them. Marion told me once that it was better to be divorced at thirty-five than never married at all. At least that one failed marriage proved some capacity for entering the union, if not actually the ability to sustain it.

'What do you mean?' I had responded to Sheryl, my first real friend in New York, during our first real lunch together. Sheryl had asked what 'defined' me. We were both twenty-seven.

'I mean just that. What defines you? What makes you you? What's your contribution to the world? How do you see yourself?'

These were very Sheryl questions. She was a kick-boxing devotee who, in her time away from her financial analyst job, studied the Kabbalah and took opera-singing and rock-climbing lessons. She saw life as one giant lab experiment that could explode at any time, but felt that was half the fun of it.

'Nothing defines me, Sheryl. I'm a very ordinary Indian girl. The only way I managed to get to this country was because my father thought it would be a good way for me to meet boys. So maybe that's what defines me. That was what it was always about, what it's still about. Getting married. You know, from the time I was seven or so, my aunt Jyoti insisted that my mother slap a homemade concoction on my face, chickpea flour mixed with lemon juice. It makes you white, you know.'

Sheryl narrowed her eyes.

'So, what went wrong?' she asked, taking in my brown complexion.

'Oh, I stopped using it. It just got to be a drag, a bit smelly and it stung. My aunt blames that for my lack of proposals. She says nobody wants a dark wife.

'You know how little girls dream of what they want to be when they grow up – an air-hostess, a movie star, a queen?' I continued. 'I used to tell my mother what my dreams were. I wanted to be a social worker, or a manicurist, I couldn't decide. I saw them both as helping people. But my mother only said, "First get married, then do what you want." I think I was twelve.

'It wasn't just me though. There was a big bunch of us girls, cousins and friends and neighbours' children, all the same age, and we went to birthday parties and ate jam sandwiches and we used to only talk about the kind of men we would marry. My best friend from school, Indu, she even had a name for her dream husband. Suresh. She liked that name. She said he would have his hair parted down the middle, and that he would be taller than her, and that she would get lots of diamonds on her wedding day, and also a big house and a fancy car. That's how she saw her life.'

'Did she get that?'

'Yup. At seventeen. A proposal that came through her aunt. They got engaged after talking for an hour in the lobby of the President Hotel, surrounded by both sets of parents. He was everything Indu said she would find, except his name was Sanjay. They have twin boys, and she rides around Bombay in the back of an air-conditioned Mercedes.'

'So, happily ever after?' Sheryl asked.

'Not really. I think he ignores her most of the time.'

I toyed with the slim gold bracelets around my wrist, and went quiet for a minute as I remembered my old friend Indu, and thought how our lives were so different now. Even she, I knew, disapproved of me.

'As soon as Indu was married, everyone started looking for a husband for me. She and I were the same age. My mother had taught me everything I needed to be a good wife, and really, I had to compensate for being so dark. So I learnt how to make perfect Indian tea, with just the right amount of condensed milk and *elaichi*. Blindfolded,

I could tell the difference between the dozens of bottles of spices on our kitchen shelves. I could make samosas, no problem. And all the Indian *bhajis*, even the complicated ones, were a breeze. They used to take me to visit people, and say, "See our daughter, all grown up now, she can do everything, cooking and all, and she's such a sensible and clever girl." In that sense, I suppose they are pretty proud of me.'

'And now, here you are. Away from all that,' Sheryl observed. 'Who would have thought it?'

Given where I had come from, and the circumstances that had brought me here, who indeed?

PART TWO

Chapter Four

The father who does not give away his daughter in marriage at the proper time is censurable.

Sources of Indian Tradition,
Volume 1, edited by W. M. Theodore de Bary

In my early twenties, I had never had any intention of leaving home before becoming someone's wife. Heading off, solo and independent, was unthinkable and irrevocably scandalous, and would effectively seal the coffin on my parents' endeavours to find me a husband.

Long before I started thinking otherwise, my mother had started us down on the more traditional path. Two days after my twenty-first birthday, she called Udhay, the most noted astrologer in Bombay. His tiny cubby-hole on the streets of Colaba – flanked by a seller of dog-eared Mills & Boon books and a hawker peddling flea-smattered limp leaf vegetables – was a regular stop-off point for Bombayites and their visiting relatives. They called on him for advice about whether to invest in a new stock, move house, when to undergo the angioplasty, should the marriage proposal be accepted.

'He's *verrrry* good,' Aunt Jyoti had said to my mother

a week earlier. 'Remember when we were having all those problems with our flat in Mysore, trying to evict the tenants? He told us on what day we should appoint the lawyer and start the legal proceedings. Believe me, Leela, within just a few weeks the problem was solved. I've been hearing *verrry* good things about him from my friends also. *Bas*, definitely you should show Anju's *chhati*. You still have her birth chart somewhere, no? Really, Leela, she's completed twenty-one now, she's graduated, but still no boys are coming for her. He'll *definitely* tell you when it will happen. Put your mind at ease, no?'

Fortunately, Udhay said that for a higher fee, he would make a house call, as my mother expressed her anxiety about being seen lingering outside his painted blue cubicle. Doubtless, *someone* would see her, and within precisely forty-five seconds, it would be all over Bombay society that there was, surely, something wrong in our family.

'Hah, hah, no problem, I'll come,' said Udhay, when my mother called him one evening. 'But vill you send me your car and driver?'

He looked educated enough. No *dhoti* around his thin brown legs or *tilok* on his forehead. Indeed, he could have been a middle-rung civil servant, in his polyester shirt and trousers, with his sun-chapped feet in tatty *chappal*s, and toting a brown leather satchel that looked as if it had barely survived World War Two.

'So, vot is the problem?' he asked, once seated, a cup of *chai* on the table next to him.

'My daughter,' said my mother, pointing to me, appropriately dressed for the occasion as I was in an unadorned cotton salwar kameez. 'She has just completed twenty-one, and my husband and I are most worried, as no boys are approaching us. Maybe there is some *grechari*?' she asked. This is a black cosmic cloud that is said to hang over the heads of the unfortunate, woebegone souls who are about to go bankrupt, lose a limb, or remain single for another year.

'Ha, ha, don't vurry, ve vill see vot is the problem,' Udhay replied, reaching into his fatigued satchel to pull out the Hindu almanac, a pad of paper and pencil and a calculator.

'Do you have her chart here?' he asked.

My mother handed over a laminated sheet covered with elaborate drawings and interspersed with the names of planets in Hindi. Udhay consulted his almanac, jotting down numbers and punching in figures on his Casio hand-held calculator, muttering under his breath.

I sat on my sweaty hands, my mother next to me, both of us quiet but anxious, the only sound in the room from the sleepy whirring of the air-conditioner behind us.

All of my friends had already been forced to have their charts read – or their mothers had done so surreptitiously – so I knew I had no choice but to sit through it. Since graduating with a bachelor's degree in commerce from Jai Hind College in nearby Churchgate, I had been having a rather grand time – or at least as grand a time as could be managed by a young girl in Bombay with a curfew and somewhat neurotic parents. But I needed to get serious about marriage, and this was the first step. So I adjusted the soft chiffon *dupatta* that was slipping off my shoulders and looked at Udhay's face for any hint of what was to come. I knew, having heard about my friends' experiences, that whatever he said in the next half-hour would set the tone for the rest of the day, indeed, the next several weeks. If the news was good – that I could and would be married within the year, to a good boy, good family, and all that, then my mother would be in such a fine and sparkling mood that my brothers would be allowed to hang out with their friends after school for at least an hour longer than usual.

I had observed, these past few months, how my mother's innate *joie de vivre* seemed slowly to diminish under the weight of her anxiety about me. She had nothing to feel sad about, surely: my father's business was thriving, allowing her to visit India Emporium to shop for Banarasi silk and French chiffon saris whenever it pleased her. Or to spend three afternoons a week playing rummy and eating *pakoda*s with her friends. Or to go along to all those religious gatherings, baby-naming ceremonies, kitty parties, where she could show off a new, shiny piece of jewellery made by my father, or talk about how well her sons were doing in school.

But invariably, she would return home from each one of these social gatherings with her elegant head slightly drooping from her graceful, South-Sea-pearl-draped neck, telling me or whoever was around that she had just heard that Shanta's son was engaged, or Mira's niece or Renu's grandson. My mother watched as all the women she grew up with, and all the distant relatives she had acquired after her marriage, were jubilant in their news of another engagement, another marriage, even another grandchild on its way. Sitting there, with her plate of *pakoda*s and her share of playing cards, contriving a smile and uttering congratulations, she always wondered why – when it came to her daughter's matrimonials – she had been dealt a bad hand.

'More tea?' I asked of Udhay, standing up to make for the kitchen, falsely believing that if I made a good impression, it might affect the outcome of things.

'*Nahin, bas,* enough,' the astrologer replied. Looking up, he said, 'I think I have understood vot is happening here.'

I caught my mother's short, whisper-quiet intake of breath, priming herself for the best news, or the worst. There were two words she would die if she heard: *anura yoga* – that the possibility of marriage does not exist.

'Your daughter has *rahu* in her seventh house,' he said, pausing. 'The timing is not good for her now for marriage. She must vait.'

'How long?' my mother asked, biting her bottom lip, her face slowly turning white, as if she were being sentenced to Alcatraz.

'Some years still,' said Udhay sorrowfully. He hated being the bearer of bad news. It often meant that the envelope containing his cash payment when he left this session would be lighter than if he had delivered happier tidings.

'*Years? Years?*' My mother was clearly stunned by his prediction. 'Months, OK, maybe, but *years*? Please, oh God, no!'

'If she had been born even twenty minutes beforehand, there vood be no problem votsoewer,' said Udhay.

Both of them looked at me as if it were my fault that I had squeezed out of my mother's womb a tad too late.

'But at the exact moment she vos born, the planets vur not fawerable. This is vy the path of matrimony is filled vith problems. There have been a few offers, *nahin*? All wrong. Maybe something wrong vith the boy. Maybe his parents are not good. Maybe your daughter doesn't like him. Maybe he doesn't like her. *Something* vill be there, in her vay. Just it von't click. Then, vun day, the path vil clear, the planets vil change, and, *bas*, your daughter will be married.'

He paused, taking another sip of his now-tepid tea.

'But only after the age of twenty-six.'

'*Hai hai*,' my mother gasped, collapsing back into the sofa. 'Twenty-six! So old? Who will want to marry her at twenty-six?' She turned to look at me, as I unthinkingly shredded a Kleenex that I'd been twisting in my perspiration-laced hands. I felt like crying, not

76

because of what the astrologer had said, but because I knew now just how much I had disappointed my mother. And it wasn't even my fault. We'd heard him – it was the planets.

'I'm sorry,' said Udhay. 'You must be patient. But hah, don't vurry, because sometimes with the right prayers and all, miracles do happen.'

'What did the astrologer say?' asked my father that night, when settled in front of the television waiting for the news on Doordharshan to start, taking his first sip of Scotch and soda.

'Nothing will happen now,' my mother replied. 'He said to wait a few more years still.' She made as if it had turned out fine – a matter of nature taking its course and all that – but, of course, I knew how she really felt.

Earlier that afternoon, after Udhay had left, my mother went into her bedroom, lay down on the silk-threaded bedspread, and quietly wept. I retreated into my room and did the same. When we both reappeared an hour later, eyes dry and clear and white again, the boys had come home from school, the television was on, the phones were ringing, the cook was asking what to make for dinner, and we both allowed the buzz and minor details of everyday life to deflect our mutual discomfort and disappointment.

My father, as it turned out, didn't particularly want to

hear the details if the feedback wasn't good. He went back to watching the news footage of a terrible train crash in Bihar.

A few weeks later, I began working at one of my father's shops. I chose the one in the Oberoi Hotel because at least there was calm and air-conditioning all around me. Plus, as my mother pointed out, 'NRIs' – non-resident Indians – often stayed in or at least shopped in the Oberoi, and often they had single sons and nephews and cousins. Being in such an environment, she had said, would help expose me to all the right people in the most fitting circumstances. My mother was nothing if not indomitable. Udhay the astrologer might have told her one thing, but astrologers could be wrong. She had heard stories of miscalculations, and perhaps my natal chart was just inaccurate. A mother had to forge on.

As it turned out, it didn't matter much what my mother's motivations were – I was happy in my new-found vocation. After a week of training at my father's Hughes Road headquarters, the largest of his five shops, I was initially given responsibility for the gold bangles section at the Oberoi boutique. Every morning at ten, after Chotu had prepared for me an omelette made with Kraft cheese and chopped parsley, I would arrive at the store, on the first floor of the hotel's shopping arcade. I dressed in a printed silk sari or embroidered salwar kameez, and took my place behind the long glass case of gleaming gold bangles. Invariably, the other sales staff would stand up when I walked in – I was the daughter of the *seth*, after all – and the guard-cum-doorman always saluted me, military-style. It still made me feel self-conscious, undeserving. This was only my 'time-pass' career, as my friends would joke. I was just doing it to while away the days until I wed.

Most of the time, there wasn't that much to do, and I knew my father was humoring me by giving me a job and paying me a thousand rupees a month, just as *karchi*, pocket money. It was cash I didn't even need as my parents always paid for everything anyway, as all parents of single girls should.

But occasionally in the afternoons it got busy, with small groups of women coming in for what they described as a 'look-see' – perhaps needing a set of gold *chooras* to give to someone as a gift. That's when the *chai-wallah* – every decent shop in India has its own resident tea-server – would flit around the store, fulfilling orders for milky tea and coffee, Bisleri mineral water and coconut juice and the tart, sugary, Limca lemon soda.

And when it was wedding season, which peaked in December, I rushed from one glass case to the next, helping show and sell chandelier-like diamond earrings, cultured pearl necklaces, bracelets covered with tiny sapphires.

'You're Gul and Leela's daughter, *nahin*?' the women

would ask, most of them pudgy and bored-looking with fairly bad taste in jewellery.

'Yes, Auntie,' I would reply, sweetly. 'Auntie, can I get you more tea?'

But my favourite moments were when the shop was quiet, and I could sit on my black velvet stool behind the gold bangles and artfully rearrange them on their stands. Slimmer, slighter ones first, then the heavier ones towards the back. Plain gold in one row, gold with silver in another, the ones with stones or enamel in another still. The tiny price-tags with their befuddling codes were nestled beneath each pair, so the eye would not be distracted from the strong, bold beauty of the shiny rounds by a miniature white label. Symmetry. A sense of order. I liked that. I polished the case outside and in, wiping away the dozens of fingerprints left by prying, trying customers. And then I would sit back and look at my work, all splendid and organized, itself a jewel. In my expansive, wealthy world, with its cars and servants and clothes, this was the only thing that truly belonged to me.

'You're *working*, is it?' asked Indu, my best friend from school, when we met for lunch a couple of days after I began my job.

'Yes, just for time-pass. Nothing wrong with it, no?'

I fiddled with the plastic chopsticks, then absent-mindedly stirred my glass of chilled *nimbu pani* while we waited for our Manchurian vegetables and spicy potato spring rolls. I looked up at Indu, who'd been my friend since we were both eight. Years ago, it had seemed an unlikely liaison. At school, I was the Chronically Awkward Girl, the one who kept tripping over her own shoelaces. I was scared to raise my hand in class, even if I thought I knew the answer, because I couldn't bear the ridicule of getting it wrong – or, worse, of having the teacher just ignore me. I was never picked for either of the teams in girls' cricket, leaving the teacher to foist me, my face burning with embarrassment, upon one of them. I was chunky then, and dark. My allergies gave me a permanently runny nose, so my mother had to pin a handkerchief to my uniform, like a banner boasting of my dysfunction. My report cards always read: 'Bright but quiet student', 'Too introverted', 'More participation needed'. I didn't understand that: I thought I was simply doing as I had been taught.

That was perhaps why I had come to see myself as one of the leftovers, the girl that would have to be fobbed off on a decent but not fabulous fellow who might take me because my daddy had money and a jewellery business. Even as a young girl, I would scan through the *The Times of India* matrimonial pages and see the ones that my parents would, at some point in the future, circle: 'Amputee, looking for spouse. No requirements.' Or 'Twice-divorced father of five needing homely woman. All offers considered.' Or the boy who gave his address as:

'Compound number three, near petrol pump.' The kind of places where worthless women ended up.

And then there was Indu. Naturally fair-skinned, always smiling, shiny hair pinned up with sparkling barrettes that her 'overseas uncle' sent her, the most popular girl in the class, the one who would have ended up heading the cheerleaders' squad, if indeed they had them in Indian convent schools. Miss Congeniality in a pretty and poised package. Everyone knew Indu would grow up to be tall-slim-fair, the girl that everyone asked for in the 'Brides Wanted' ads.

I had felt pretty insignificant until the day Indu came shimmering into my life. I had been sitting alone on a stone bench in the playground, eating chutney sandwiches and drinking diluted orange cordial from a Thermos. Indu came along and took my hand and led me to the hopscotch place, and never quite let me go. Even when we drifted apart at seventeen – as I went to college, and Indu got married – we were, as everyone called us: 'best girlie-friends'.

Today, at lunch, I looked at my friend, with her still fair skin and same shiny hair. She was plumper now, after recently bearing twin boys, but still resplendent in the mundane environment of the Chow Chow Maharaja restaurant. Even so, she seemed to be smiling less.

'How's Sanjay?' I asked of her husband.

'Hah, fine, busy, travelling.' The remnants of her smile quickly dissipated.

'Nice earrings,' I remarked, looking at the three-carat heart-shaped solitaires that shone from her perfect white earlobes.

'Thank you.' The smile returned. 'From him, after the twins were born. I know we should have bought them from your daddy's shop, but he found these on a business trip in Belgium. Pretty, no?' As is considered proper even among young wives, Indu never referred to her husband by his first name. It was always 'he', a word that was hushed out from her lips with an almost reverential air.

'So,' Indu continued, turning the conversation to me. 'Any boys? Any good offers?'

We saw each other every week, talked almost every day, and she always asked the same question. There was, after all, nothing else for her to inquire about, since she wasn't particularly interested in my new job. With the exception of Bina, whose husband had left her after only two months of marriage, I was the only one still single.

'Actually, Indu, no, no boys, no offers. Udhay, you know that astrologer everyone goes to, well he came over last week and read my *chhati* and said it would take some time yet. Bad planets.'

'Yes, even I went to Udhay before my marriage,' said Indu. 'Everything he said came true.'

My heart collapsed.

'He told me I would be engaged before eighteen, it would be an arranged match, that my husband would have something to do with steel manufacturing, that he

83

would be only a few years older than me, and handsome and all. See, all happened,' she said, smug and satisfied.

I glanced down at my friend's slender white fingers, tips coloured a brilliant pink, amazingly unchipped given she had two infant boys. (It must have had to do with the fact that the feeding, changing and washing were all left to others.) Then my eye fell on Indu's engagement ring, which, as per custom, she still wore above her wedding band. A pear-shaped rock the size of a baby cockroach, sitting atop a gold band embedded with round diamonds. I always loved looking at other girls' rings, imagining the moment when they were slipped on by the men in question, wondering what both people were thinking, how they felt, if they cherished the face in front of them. I yearned for a pair of rings like that on my own somewhat darker, chubbier finger. I could help myself to any one of thousands of such trinkets courtesy of my father. But I wanted a man to lightly hold up my right hand, look at my face with love and longing, and gently slide the rings on.

'Tell me, Indu, when you first met Sanjay, did you know that he was the one?'

Despite being best friends, I had never asked this question before. When your seventeen-year-old 'best girlie-friend' gets engaged, all you can do is gush and start planning the trousseau and the parties.

'Of course,' she said, mildly defensively. 'What would

84

make him not the one? He was the first boy my parents showed me. And he was everything Udhay said he would be. Of course.'

'Did you love him immediately?'

'Yes, immediately. So handsome, so tall, so nice, and with the gifts and all. And remember our wedding?' Indu drifted off somewhere. 'More than eight hundred people at the Taj Crystal Ballroom. His parents gave me everything. They were scared, you know, that he would go off with that Indian Airlines air-hostess, *chori*, and so when he said yes to me, how happy they were.'

'But you were so young and beautiful,' I reasoned. 'You could have waited, no?'

'Wait for what?' A mist of irritation gathered behind her eyes. 'To become old and single, like you? I'll tell you one thing. The longer you wait, the harder it becomes. Now you have become a working girl. It doesn't matter that you are working in your daddy's company, boys still don't like it. Better you stop that, go to more *satsang*s with your mother. See now, wedding season is starting. Many boys will come to Bombay. Their mothers will see you serving *chai* in the shop. It's very bad. Doesn't matter what Udhay said, you must still *try*. But how can you pay attention to such things if you're busy helping people try on bangles the whole day?'

I wanted to cry. In all our years of friendship, there had never been an outburst like this. Usually, Indu was lacking in any opinions about anything. She was even a bit vacuous in a pleasant sort of way. I had never seen her resentful.

I looked down at the Manchurian vegetable leftovers and the bowls of cold rice that sat between us, to avoid catching her eye. For what I'd just seen in my best friend's face was the same look that I had seen in my parents', in Udhay's, in all the people working in the shop and those who came in every day, even the ancient security guard who stood up every morning to salute me.

The look in their eyes might have been anything.

But I was quite sure it was pity.

Chapter Five

Hinduism does not support using occultism for selfish motives and dissuades everyone from meddling with occultism.

Am I a Hindu? by Ed Viswanathan

'*What* are we to do with her?' my mother asked plain-tively, her head covered with her *dupatta*, as she sat at the feet of her guru.

Swami Upananda was cross-legged on an armchair, towering above his disciple, his eyes closed beneath the bushels that doubled as brows.

He was deep in meditation, consulting with the God he insisted was living within him, passing forth to Him the questions followers came to ask. The insides of his wide, black nostrils were lined with grey hairs, tufts of which also shot out of his droopy ears. His head was shaved clean every day – an act he believed atoned for the sins committed in all his prior lives. Small warts, like flecks of chocolate chips, studded the surface of his brown, sag-ging, eighty-year-old cheeks. Now, his eyes were closed and his cracked lips slowly started to part, small droplets of spittle gathering in each corner of his mouth.

My mother looked around the living room – the piles of yellowed, crackling, dusty Marathi newspapers in one corner, the day-bed opposite. Behind her, a dozen or so other people waited their turn to talk to their Swamiji, craning their necks and straining to hear what was being said to anyone in front of them.

My mother was now as familiar with this living room as with her own, so often had she made the journey here, an hour's drive to the outskirts of Bombay. She had come in the past, not just for me, but also when Anand had had a bout of bronchitis and when Anil's grades had faltered. Swami Upananda had proffered some blessed food for the afflicted brother to eat, and wrote down a mantra for the lazy one to chant. It had always worked, although my mother had never quite allowed for the possibility that Anand's illness had subsided with ordinary doctor-prescribed medication, and that Anil had started doing much better with his term papers because he didn't want to chant any mantras.

But today, my mother had spent twenty minutes telling her Swamiji all about the daughter who wasn't getting any good marriage offers, that she was certain a curse had befallen the family, that all her friends were gossiping and her relatives were feeling sorry for her and that, frankly, she had had enough and there must be *something*, surely, that he could do. He had cured people of cancer and blindness, so it was said. He was especially adept at beating evil spirits out of people – the spirits that would jump into unsuspecting folk who walked beneath the whispering old trees at night, something that we grew up knowing never to do.

Now, his eyes closed, Swami Upananda was in a trance. He would soon return to full consciousness, bringing with him an oracle from the Divine Light within.

My father, also seated cross-legged, heard a soft exhalation emanating from the holy man's nostrils.

'He's asleep,' my father whispered to my mother. 'You're telling him your life story, and, *bas*, he's gone to sleep.'

My mother raised her hand to tug at her guru's orange robe – she hadn't come all this way in mid-afternoon traffic for nothing – and he startled awake.

'Hah, Leela-*behen*,' he said, addressing her as a sister. 'Daughter remains unmarried. *Verry* bad. I have asked the Gods for advice, and they say that yes, there is a curse upon you, a terrible *grechari*, put upon you by a relative long ago, now passed on.'

She knew it. It *had* to be something that somebody else had done. They had been model, marriage-minded parents, and had raised a model, marriage-minded daughter – if one that could stand to lose a few pounds, get her eyebrows threaded more frequently and actually use the Promise of Fairness cream.

'You will have no problems with your sons, they will marry fast fast,' said the Swami. This was not exactly news. 'Fair-tall-handsome boys, well settled, when their time comes there will be plenty of girls.'

'But who put this curse on, Swamiji?' my mother asked. 'And why? Why on my daughter?'

'Hmmmm.' The holy one closed his eyes for a second, trying to think of an answer, but he seemed slightly distracted by the smell and sizzle of frying *pakoda*s wafting in from the kitchen next door. 'Some cousin of your husband, long ago. She wanted to marry him, you see. And, *bas*, when he married you, she became most angry. She went to her grave a *nyaarni*, a virgin. And she put a curse on your head that your first-born would never marry.'

'*Hai!*' my mother gasped, sinking into the floor. '*Never marry! That she'll never marry!* But, Swamiji, please, there must be something we can do, *nahin*?'

'Of course, Leela-*behen*. When God and I are present, what curses can come true? When you have prayer and you appease the Gods, how can they not listen to you? There are plenty plenty things to do.'

My mother reached into her handbag for a pen and a scrap of paper, while my father hurried her along. He wanted to be home in time for the World Wrestling Federation semi-finals on TV.

'*Beti*, I went to see Swamiji today, and everything will be fine,' my mother cooed to me that evening. 'See, there's a *grechari* but now it can be cleared, just a few small things for you to do, very easy. Are you hungry, *beti*?'

I had had a good day at the shop, having sold twenty-one pairs of bangles, a record for me. They were all bought by the same person, a somewhat rude and overbearing woman whose son was about to be married and who needed identical gifts for all the relatives so there would be no squabbling among them. I was proud of myself, having done all the negotiating and selling. I knew the other salespeople had been impressed with how I handled it, and by now, surely my father would have heard of my triumph.

'Hah, Ma, I'm hungry, didn't have any time to eat my lunch today, so busy in the shop.' I handed over the metal tiffin that one of the servants brought to me on the days I didn't want to come home for lunch. 'Maybe Chotu can just heat this up and I'll have some of it now as a snack and wait for Daddy to come home to eat proper dinner, *nahin*?'

A few minutes later, changed into my 'rough use' salwar kameez, I was seated in front of the television watching that day's re-run of *The Bold and the Beautiful*, my favourite American soap. I dipped a re-heated *chapatti* into okra curry and waited to see who Ridge was going to sleep with today.

My mother came and sat next to me.

'Swamiji has given a small mantra for you to say, and has suggested a simple fast,' said my mother. She seemed particularly uninterested in Ridge's love life, not surprising given her laser focus on mine, I suppose.

'*Ek* minute, Ma, the programme has almost finished.'

As the ending credits rolled, and the familiar jangling music started up, I turned off the television, set down my plate, licked the remnants of the curry from my fingers and turned my attention to my mother.

'You can start this coming Monday,' she said. 'Monday is Lord Shiva's day, the best day for starting any prayers or pujas. Here, Swamiji gave me this for you.' My mother unfolded her hand to reveal a pale green *mala*, a long rosary. 'There are one hundred and one beads on this. You must say the mantra on each bead, and go around eleven times, every morning after bathing. Understood?'

I did a quick calculation in my head, and worked out that I would be spending the rest of my twenties chanting the mantra, thus obviating the need for a husband or any social life whatsoever.

'You need to pray more, *beti*. Swamiji says you're not praying enough,' my mother continued.

'And from where did he hear that?' I asked. 'Does he come into this house every day to see how much time each one of us is spending in the *mandir*? How does he know when I pray and when I don't?'

'He just knows, *beti*. He knows everything. He is a master. Now just do this *mala* every day, and start the Shiva fast, and all will be fine.'

I knew the procedure, even if I hadn't been through it myself. Most of my female friends had kept a weekly Monday fast as soon as they came of marriageable age. Everyone, of course, with the exception of Indu, whose nuptials were enviably hassle- and thus fasting-free.

It wasn't that arduous: only fruit and milk from sunrise to sunset. At that point, the fast could be broken, with the consumption of a strictly vegetarian meal, which was in itself so gargantuan that the girls invariably ended up putting on weight as a result of fasting. I used to see them at various parties and gatherings, sitting in one corner, all with their perfectly arched eyebrows and polished fingernails and forced smiles and 'yes, Auntie, thank you, Auntie' nodding heads. And all the aunties and mothers would shine with approval, see my Lata/Gita/Nina/Nita, such a good girl, fasting, so Shiva will be happy and bring her a good boy.

I had known then that it would only be a matter of time before I was asked to give up a weekly meal – two, if you count breakfast – plus any snacks I would ordinarily treat myself to. But it wasn't until Swami Upananda proposed it that my mother decided it was time.

'Fine, Ma, whatever you want,' I said. I wasn't in the mood to argue, and besides, it was no big deal – just once a week, and it would keep my mother happy.

Or so I thought.

*　　*　　*

My mother became a woman possessed by the Demon of Husband-Hunters. In the months that followed, she and my father took me on four pilgrimages across India and to visit any swami/saint/guru/healer/astrologer she could drum up. We drove for six hours to get to Shirdi, flew to Puttaparthi, trekked to Vaishnudevi and rattled along by railway to Rishikesh and Haridwar.

Everywhere, I bowed my head at the feet of living saints or to marble statues of them. I ate vast amounts of *prasad*, sang *bhajan*s in my off-key voice, watched as my parents handed over donations to temples to buy blessings.

All I wanted to do was go sell my bangles and then come home in the evenings to watch the various members of the Forrester family clamber in and out of bed with one another. I wanted to hang out with my friends – even if they were by now all married couples – for films at the Eros cinema, and afterwards go for ice cream at Yankee Doodle. There, the wind would sometimes sweep the frozen, sugary, creamy pistachio-flavoured scoop off its wafer cone, like a mushy green tumbleweed, leaving everyone giggling. At those moments, it didn't matter that I wasn't married. I was still part of a group.

But now, those times when I felt somewhat free and moderately uplifted were rare. I wasn't allowed to believe that my life was fine and acceptable as it was. Instead, I had to strive for something that I knew I really didn't have much control over. There were times when I would cry in my room at some remark that my mother might make about another girl. 'So what if she's fat/sad/stupid? At least she's married.' The pressure that society put on my mother, she transferred onto me. I found it hard to blame her; she was an Indian mother, and she knew no other way. The worry I saw on her face, I knew was because of me. The sadness in her eyes – all me. All I wanted to do was to allow her to feel joy, and bring her some peace. And the only way I could do that was to give her a son-in-law. Without that, her life was meaningless. And so was mine.

Even so, my girlfriends insisted that yes, prayer can do the most amazing things.

'My mama did the same for me, but we started a bit earlier,' said Lata, a childhood friend, as I joined four couples and Lata's teenage brother to play Scrabble one Sunday afternoon. 'Really, something will just work, maybe one of the *sant*s you go see will give you just the right mantra. We're always hearing of such miracles,' said Lata. As she reassured me, I noticed that her husband had been using his hands to rub away dead skin from between his toes just before offering around *dokhla*s with his fingers.

I missed many such gatherings as my mother toted me from one miracle-worker to the next. There was Sai Baba's ashram in Puttaparthi, in the hills high above Bangalore, where we had to leave our roach-infested room at four in the morning to make it for *darshan* fifteen minutes later. We sat at the back of a two-thousand-strong group of people, all there, like us, for blessings, waiting for the avatar – God on earth – to appear from his gold-gated palace. He was said to keep all his powers in the frizzy black halo of hair that surrounded his smiling face, and as he walked, rose petals and holy ash dripped from his palms – divine manifestations, everyone said. Sai Baba traversed the wide circle around his courtyard, his helpers keeping the seated masses at bay, and occasionally leaned forward to pluck a letter from someone's outstretched hand. It was said that if he read the note, the prayers contained therein would be answered. My mother had her missive tucked away in her bag, just in case she made it anywhere near the front of the group. So far, abundant donations notwithstanding, she never had.

A month later, I accompanied my mother and Aunt Jyoti to the Balaji Temple, a rugged, uneven edifice set atop the hills above Madras. Long queues had formed from dawn, with thousands of people here to seek fulfillment of their prayers. It was a different system here – there were no letters nor any brandishing of powdery, mysterious ash. Here, devotees indicated their heart's desire by choosing from a pile of tiny figurines and depositing them into an open basket that lay at the feet of a statue of the deity Balaji. There were miniature houses and cars and babies; I had been told there were even some of an American green card. My mother asked the man behind the counter for a token symbolizing the marriage of her daughter, and he handed over a tiny wooden man, the kind you would find at the top of a wedding cake. Ironically, this one was unsmiling and badly dressed – the kind of marriage prospects I'd been turning up lately. So at least it was an accurate depiction.

Three hours later, after waiting for our turn in the endless queue, we spent a total of twelve seconds dropping the wooden figure into the wicker basket and uttering a small prayer, our three dark-haired heads bowed in unison.

It was soon determined that the Monday fast wasn't powerful enough. Within three months, I had been coerced into taking on a weekly Thursday ritual. Subsequently, I tagged on a special, super-duper Friday fast, one in honour of the great Goddess Santoshi Ma, alter-ego of Lakshmi, the grande dame of all goddesses. It was a sixteen-week fast, far more rigorous and complicated than the others, and it more or less put an end to my Scrabble-playing, film-watching social life.

Plus, I had to wear the marriage-inducing accoutrements: the black thread on my right wrist assigned by one guru, the silver talisman that hung from my neck given to me by another. There was the four-carat coral, the colour of a sun-ripened orange, affixed to a dull gold ring which

I was directed to wear on the fourth finger of my right hand. And a pale yellow sapphire set in silver to be worn on the index finger of my left hand. Both had been suggested by yet another astrologer who divined that these stones would help redirect the planetary energies around me.

As I jingled and jangled around, I thought that it was a very good thing that my father owned a jewellery store.

In the midst of all this piety and pilgrimage-going, I changed. I began to feel quite fantastically blameless. My family looked upon me as their striving, sincere daughter, the one who would battle karmic ills and emerge victorious, brandishing a good husband as the prize for all the starving and chanting and beseeching of the Gods. I felt tepid, passive, inconsequential. I had acquired an attitude of fatalism – what will be, will be, but in the meantime we must do our part. And, like my mother, I became solely focused on the pursuit of marriage, instead of on the grasping and enjoyment of life as it presented itself to me every day.

Each morning, I watched my mother do prayer rituals in our small temple at home, where she would wash the tiny statuettes of Ganesh, Lakshmi and Shiva with milk and rose water, and dress them in fabric swatches that had tiny holes cut out for the head, like minuscule ponchos. Then she would sing the *aarti*: '*Om jai jagdish hare*' – 'Oh glory be to God'. I would go in there, and soak up the smell of incense and the melted ghee which had been used to light the devotional flame. Like my mother, I too prayed for some resolution.

Chapter Six

Discrimination between the sexes in India begins at birth, or even before it. It starts before the child is born, in the mother's womb. None of the conventional blessings showered upon a pregnant woman mentions daughters.'

Caste as Woman, by Vrinda Nabar

Three years passed. And still, each day, from ten in the morning to six in the evening, I sank into the safety of my air-conditioned, black velvet world. Coming to work in my father's jewellery shop was the only proof that I even existed. Beyond that, I was merely some solitary astrological anomaly.

Even my friends, Indu included, had become more and more distant, involved in their own married lives and expanding circles of coupled-off friends. The young wives all began to look the same, indulging in the latest thing – golden brown highlights in their hair one month, coloured contact lenses the next – all with a view to hiding real parts of themselves. Their husbands generally seemed fatter every time I saw them, on each occasion becoming less and less the dashing young boys their wives had married.

To add to my mounting loneliness, the letters had

started coming. Anand had been the first in the entire clan to go off for what the rest of the family and community described as 'further studies' at UCLA, in sunny, spirited California. He was enrolled in an engineering programme, had settled in nicely. In addition to the telephone calls which would generate much excitement and anxiety at home ('Anand, *beta*, is everything OK? Are you eating good food? Are you being a good boy?' my mother exhorted), his letters were filled with adventures: his outings with his new best friend Pawan, who happened to be from Delhi. The second-hand BMW he had just bought. The Saturday afternoons on Venice Beach. The yummy-sounding raspberry smoothie from Jamba Juice. ('Hah, smoothie,' my mother had responded. 'Sounds like a *lassi* only.') In his missives and down that tinny long-distance phone line, he always sounded breezy and free and buoyant. Of course, all my mother wanted to know was how old Pawan was, and, once told he was only nineteen, if he perhaps had any older brothers? Cousins, even?

With each epistle, I felt increasingly demoralized. Anil, the older of my two brothers, was happily ensconced in the family business. At twenty-two, he was playing the role of rich young lad, out with what our parents called 'other youngsters'. He was a central, crucial cog in a smooth operation of fun friends and acquaintances, some of them, too, slowly pairing off. The girls would call – Manju and Priya and Pinky and Veena – gurgling to my mother: 'Hello, Auntie, is Anil home?' They phoned under the guise of friendship but everyone knew that they all wanted to marry him. Sometimes their mothers would call too, and drop little hints here and there. Anil just laughed and good-naturedly played along with it. He was young, and not in any rush.

Which left me feeling ever more isolated.

'Mama, doesn't anyone ever call to ask for me?' I asked my mother one day, after she had received a phone call from Auntie Barkha wondering if perhaps Anil 'was ready'.

'No,' my mother replied, not sensing the need to cosset my feelings. '*Bas*, you've been sitting so long, everyone knows you. Not like those other new new girls who are just coming out. Those are the girls everyone wants, nah?'

'Hah, Ma,' I whispered, slithering back to my room.

I knew, however, the precise moment that my mother's desperation had reached its pinnacle. The two of us were walking down Colaba Causeway one Saturday – one of the few days left in the week when I wasn't fasting – when she stopped and began staring at a dirty, half-demolished wall. On it was a tattered pink poster, advertising the services of one Parmeshwar Dutta, a matchmaker in Andheri. Her Unique Selling Point appeared to be: 'No matrimonial case too hard! All matches can be found! Give us the impossible, and we will make it possible!' When I saw my mother scribbling down the accompanying phone number on the back of her hand, I knew it was time to get out. Things might have been bad, but not so bad that I was going to find a husband from an old flyer on a street corner.

Chapter Seven

A handsome, light-skinned boy is generally preferred, especially if the girl is beautiful ... The boy must be a 'nice person', well brought up and not a potential wife-beater.

Village Life in Northern India by Oscar Lewis

My brother Anil had become, far and away, the most sought-after bachelor in Bombay. Of course, he had always been a bit of a bright shining star. But now that he was inching into his early twenties, the stakes were higher. Where before there was lingering attention paid to him, now those aunties and their daughters were fixing their focus. He was it. He was the one that everyone wanted. I should have been happy for him, I suppose. But, through absolutely no fault of his own, as his cachet rose, mine fell.

Each time one of those phone calls came, he attempted to leave the room. He started moving from his space on the sofa, the one closest to the television, as soon as he heard our mother's voice change – ever so slightly but ever so noticeably – when she picked up the receiver.

'Oh, *hellooo*,' she would say. '*How* are you? *How*

is your husband?' We knew it was one of her card-playing, kitty-group-going friends, the ones with the eligible daughters and nieces, the ones who looked at Anil as a boy whose time for matrimony had come. Her voice changed because she knew, instinctively, once the receiver was up by her bejewelled ear, that this was not a call to invite her to another cocktail party, another wedding. It was her special voice, the one rich and replete with equal parts pride and humility. People had begun calling from everywhere. Why, just yesterday, her friend Lata from London had sent her a photograph of one particularly thoroughbred girl, tall and fair and slim and rich. The girl was surrounded by others, in a picture obviously taken at a ladies' luncheon. But a bright pink Post-It note, an arrow inked on its front, pointed to the candidate in question. On it were scribbled details: 'Nineteen, vegetarian, devotee of Sai Baba, five feet five inches, home-loving girl.'

'Perfect for Anil,' Lata had written in a separate note. 'I am sure he will like my niece very much.'

But while my mother courted the attention, she simultaneously mentally held out her hands, telling everyone to stop, please. Her boy would not be getting married just yet as she had an older daughter first, still single, 'still sitting'. The strategy was to remain polite and willing and open, as she would never know when the planets would commute on their mysterious course, uplifting their shadows from my single state and I would be wed. Immediately after, she had resolved, it would be Anil's turn.

Or perhaps, she reasoned, one of the mothers and aunts might be inspired to drum up a candidate for me, as a way of getting in with our family.

'Of course, I *understand* that,' said Jyoti during one of their thirty-two daily conversations. 'Of course I understand that you want to see your daughter married first. Which parent doesn't? But Anil is *soooo* good. He's *sooo* ready, I can tell. He's what, twenty-two? A very fine age for marriage for boys. See, Gopi's son, Vikram. Only twenty-one and he's engaged already. But such a *lovely* girl he got. So if you're getting offers from such good girls for Anil, you *must* consider it, Leela. These girls get taken very quickly, and then there will be nobody left for him. Do you want him to become like your daughter? Alone and unmarried?'

I could tell that my mother wanted to fight to resurrect my good name, but today didn't have the strength to combat her sister's domination over the family's matrimonial landscape. Jyoti could afford to proffer advice. Her own two girls, Nina and Namrata, were still teenagers, but everyone knew that as soon as they were ready to cross the marriage threshold, there would be plenty of boys waiting. They were *good* girls.

In truth, I didn't want my brother to marry before me. I didn't want to be the older, single sister, smiling on the outside and crying within, the girl sleeping in the small

113

bedroom closest to the front door while my brother and his new bride cuddled happily in their suite.

'Let's wait and see,' said my mother, quietly. 'My poor daughter. I can't just forget about her. I'm praying hard that something will happen for her soon. And better to wait for her. Once my boys start getting married, everyone will think that I've given up on her and no one will come forward for her any more.'

'Yes,' said Jyoti. 'But is anyone coming forward for her now? Hah? When was the last time you got a proposal for her? Must have been some years back, no? See, Leela, sometimes when a marriage happens in the family, it opens the door for destiny. It is like bang bang bang, all blockages are cleared. Maybe I'm younger than you, Leela, and maybe my daughters are still not ready for marriage, but these things I know. Listen to me. Get Anil married.'

When I was tired of socializing with my own coupled-off friends, I accompanied Anil on his social forays, just for a change of pace. He and his gang hung out at Shamiana, the coffee shop in the Oberoi Hotel. We clucked on about this and that, fidgeting with the assortment of glasses of *lassi* and *nimbu pani* and dishes of chicken *chaat* and *bhel puri* that littered the table.

'So, what's the latest movie, *yaar*?' asked Vikram, newly engaged and due to be wed. His shy fiancée Mira, hand-picked by Vikram's mother, sat demurely by his side.

114

'Everyone is saying *Die Hard* is excellent,' replied Janak, Anil's closest friend from school. 'Shall we try and catch it?'

'I'm happy just sitting here,' said Lavina, part of the group, her chin cupped in her soft, white hands, their nails painted a non-threatening shade of pink, as she gazed at Anil through long lashes. It was patently obvious she liked him, but it was not something she could discuss with any of the other girls at the table, as they were all pursuing him too.

Janak sat back in his chair and surveyed the scene quietly, smiling. He was mostly ignored by the girls, probably because he was a little on the chubby side. That really wouldn't have mattered to them had he the bank balance of the other boys at the table. He didn't have that, either.

I had to confess though, Lavina *was* cute. And she seemed nice and sincere, not like the others who even came out to a casual dinner looking as if they were about to take part in the Miss World evening gown competition. Oh, God, is Mamta really wearing *glitter* in her hair?

Anil and I got home just after eleven that night, having gone to see *Die Hard* after all. We both slipped off our shoes at the entrance, and I was reminded by him to touch the feet of the marble Ganesh in the hallway, something he never forgot to do. We heard the gentle buzz of the television in the living room, the rustling of newspapers, our parents' voices.

'Hi, Mama, Dad,' he said.

'Did you have a good time?' our mother asked. 'Want some hot pista milk before you go to sleep?'

'*Nahin*, thank you,' Anil replied, as we both plopped down tiredly on the couch. 'I ate a lot at dinner and then just had a Thumbs-Up at the movie, so I'm full.' He stretched out his long, lean, jeans-clad legs. We were both avoiding one of *those* conversations.

'So, who was there?' asked our mother. 'Who came to dinner?'

'Oh, just the usual,' Anil replied nonchalantly. 'Janak, Mamta, Shalu and Pooja. Vikram and Mira. And Lavina.'

'Hah? Lavina was there? Her mummy spoke to me today . . .'

'And so?' she continued. 'What news about Vikram and Mira's wedding? That will be a big, big wedding, no?' She turned to look at my father, dozing off in his chair. 'I've heard that Mira has already started looking around at the best boutiques in Bombay and Delhi, asking designers to make her outfits for all the parties. And they are using a film producer, imagine, a film producer, to organize the functions! So grand! Someone told me they are planning to do a black-and-white theme party, and another one for fancy dress. So nice, no? So lucky for their mothers, to be able to plan such fun fun parties. And the wedding is going to be at the Turf Club, outdoors on the grass,

116

under plenty plenty lights and a hundred stalls serving different foods. She's a *boootiful* girl – nah? – that Mira. She'll look *soooo* pretty!'

'Yes, Ma,' said Anil quietly. 'But we didn't really talk about all that at dinner.'

'And *yes*! I hear Mira's parents are buying her at least six different jewellery sets to match all her party clothes. South Sea pearls one day, emeralds the next. I'm sure they will also come to our shop, nah?' she asked, again looking over at my father, who by now was snoring.

'And I'm sure they will give Vikram a good dowry, he's *such* a good boy from a nice family. Everyone is saying there will be at least a three-carat ring for him, and some fancy watch, Cartier-Bartier. Not that he needs, hah? Vikram's family is also rich rich. They will also give plenty,' my mother reasoned, finally sitting back.

'*Beta*, what about Lavina for you?' she asked my brother suddenly, randomly, the words tumbling out of her mouth before she had the chance to rein them in. 'Her mummy spoke to me today. You are friends, nah? You like her?'

I might as well not have been there, so little did I matter in this conversation.

'She's OK, Ma,' Anil replied. 'But I'm still young, so let's wait a little, no? Plus . . .' He turned to look at me, and then fell silent. I wasn't sure if I had become a handy excuse for not rushing into marriage or if he was genuinely concerned about my state of mind.

'Ay, when will things happen for you?' my mother wailed, tearlessly, finally turning to look at me, her head shaking slowly, a lock of lacquered hair falling down over one eye. She pinched nervously at the buttons of her pink polyester kaftan and turned to look at Anil. '*Beta*, I don't know how long we can wait. See, even your friends are getting married now. At least you, you are still young, you can find a good, pretty girl. If you wait, even you will become too old, all the good girls will get married, and there will be nothing left for you. I don't like at all the idea of seeing poor Anju *nyaarni*, still single, at your wedding. I will cry to see that. So we must all move on, try our best. No?'

The alliance between Vikram and Mira was the talk of all Bombay, if only because of the sheer volume of money that would be lavished at the nuptials, which had already been set to take place a year from now. That would give everyone involved sufficient time to plan the *shaadi* to end all *shaadi*s. Emeralds and satins, imported entertainment and jet-fresh flowers – it was going to be a supreme blockbuster, all conceived of and implemented by a top Bollywood producer on a lucrative and frenzied freelance mission. This was, after all, going to be a fantasy event.

Romantically, however, this did not appear to be one of those written-in-the-stars encounters. Instead the betrothal was exceedingly matter-of-fact: Mira was a girl known to Vikram and his family. They had gone out, she and he and a group of friends, from time to time and got to know one another in that sweet and superficial way that young people do. As far as matches go, they didn't come more ideal than this. It was 'part love, part arranged', everyone teased. Neither family could have asked for a better coupling.

'I suppose we clicked, *yaar*,' Vikram had told us a few days after the engagement was announced. 'Sweet girl. Cute-looking, no? And quiet, no trouble. My parents and her parents are good friends, our mummies play cards every week. She had turned twenty, finished college, and her parents knew it was time. I was working with Dad, settled in my job. So when the proposal came, I didn't have a reason to say no. I mean,' he added quickly, 'I wanted to say yes. Yes, I wanted to say yes.'

We were all having dinner at Vikram's house in Juhu, near the sea, where the open tracts of land and salty air permit a more slumbering pace of life than in the rest of Bombay. Vikram had never had to worry about not finding a girl. Since he was seventeen, his mother's friends – all those ladies he had charmingly called 'auntie auntie' since he was a little boy – had kept chaste young girls in mind for him. And why not? Lots of money there – made from steel, shipping, supermarkets – and yes, he was a nice-looking boy. A bit on the short side, but quite nice-looking none the less.

'So, in the end, it was like a coffee-shop arrangement,

hah?' I asked Vikram, as we slurped the remains of our *kulfi falooda* from small sterling silver cups. 'You and Mira sat down in Shamiana with her parents and yours, and you all decided amongst yourselves that it was time for you and her to get engaged. It wasn't like, you know, you just really fell for her or anything, was it?'

'Come on,' Vikram replied, setting down his cup so it tinkled as it hit the glass coffee table. 'What do you mean "fell for"? She's sweet, and she has a cute figure. Mummy and Daddy are happy. She'll fit in with the household. Why say no?'

I had been there when this much-envied couple cemented the betrothal. There was a small ceremony in a high-ceilinged red-carpeted room that served as the family temple in Vikram's home. It was only immediate relatives and close friends – a mere 120 people. Vikram and Mira exchanged floral garlands, and put 'unofficial' rings on one another's fingers (just a temporary stop-gap until the 'official' engagement which would take place a week before the wedding – I never quite understood the logic of that).

Later, Mira's closest friends huddled with her in one corner.

'You're *sooo* lucky, Mira!' they gushed.

'Vikram is *rrrreally* nice! Let's see the ring! Wah-wah! At least four carats, and *such* a good colour diamond! And it's only the *kachi misri*. Just wait until the real *misri*!'

Mamta and Pooja, Shalu and Lavina were all gurgling

deliriously. Mira was proud. She was the first in her little nucleus of girlfriends to get engaged. She had set a precedent. He was rich and cute, if short, but she was considered petite, so that all worked out for the best. She had done well. And now she could go shopping and buy saris and jewellery and plan lots of parties.

It was the wedding that was important.

The marriage, frankly, was secondary.

'I want to go to America,' I said to my father the next morning, as we all sat down to breakfast.

'Umrica? Hah, OK, plenty of people there you can visit and stay with. It's a very good idea. Plenty of boys there, no? Maybe you can go for a month or so. Go to New Jersey and stay with Uncle Lal. He'll be most happy to look after you.'

'Actually, Dad, I was thinking I want to go and study there. Like Anand is doing.'

Anil and my parents all stopped eating. Clearly, they thought I had been possessed by one of those spirits that lurk in the trees at night. 'Are you crazy? What a nonsense idea!' my father shouted. He was mostly a quiet-tempered man, and only became inflamed when there was some attack on his honour, integrity, reputation or intelligence.

'Daddy,' I pleaded, sitting on my sweaty palms and biting my bottom lip, like I always did when I was nervous, 'just think about it. All my friends are married, I feel quite alone, and I'm not doing anything here really. Nothing useful or worthwhile. During the day I go to the shop to do a job that anyone can do, and nobody takes me seriously over there, because I'm only your daughter.'

'What do you mean?' my mother asked, disbelief shadowing her eyes. 'You are working happily in Daddy's shop, meeting people. You come with me here and there to parties and shopping. You have your friends, like Indu and all. You will soon find a boy, yes, yes. What do you mean you are not doing anything here?'

She hadn't heard a word that I had said.

Anil finally spoke.

'Mama, Daddy, Anand has gone for further studies, so you can't tell Anju no. And things have changed now, girls are becoming more independent. See Priya, Uncle Lachu and Auntie Rekha's daughter, she has also gone for hotel school in Switzerland. We have to be more open.'

I smiled gratefully at my brother: for a young spoilt Indian boy, he was remarkably evolved.

'But, *beti*, you are already educated,' my mother said, calming down, hoping that reasoning with me would return me to my senses. 'You got your B.Com. already. And what will all the people say? That Gul and Leela's daughter, still unmarried, is going alone to Umrica. How will you find a boy if you become a student again? And then when you come back here, educated and all, who will want you?'

I felt like I was going to cry, but I couldn't afford to. For if I started now, I would never stop. They would be the tears of a girl who should have been born a boy.

I had always known that, yet never spoken of it.

That, ultimately, was what it had always come down to. My parents, when they were newly married, were supposed to have a male heir. How could they not? They were youthful, handsome, growing rich, two of the community's favourite people, and the only blessing that remained for them now would be the birth of a son.

My mother knew it as soon as she was told she was pregnant; it was going to be a boy and she said as much to everyone. She would name him Avinash – what a strong, solid name! And a bottle of Johnnie Walker Black Label whisky would be sent to each of their friends, along with a kilo of fresh pistachios and a box of Quality Street chocolates, imported from England. It would be a celebration, a perfect finale, and at the same time the start of her new family. She couldn't wait for the contractions to start.

And then I slid out, with a minuscule slit instead of the worm-like appendage she had been looking forward to seeing. Oh God, she had delivered a *daughter* as a first-born. The unthinkable had happened. Her in-laws would never forgive her.

It's not hard to know when you're a disappointment. I was the consolation prize. It was the same for so many girls I knew, except for those who came after a son had already arrived. As much as our parents reassured us otherwise, we were all trussed-up detritus.

Marrying young and marrying well would have been a way of making it up to my parents. And I couldn't even get that right. Instead, I became the too-dark, too-plump one, the one with the turbulent inner life. There had to be *something* better out there for me: a life wherein I didn't feel like such a disappointment; people who saw something in me that nobody here in Bombay saw.

'Please, Daddy, please,' I said, dispensing with the speech I had prepared, the answers to the questions I knew my father would ask. 'Let me just try it,' I whispered.

'Over my dead body,' my father said, his anger rising again. 'I will not permit it.'

Chapter Eight

This individual striving after ever higher educational qualifications and after higher social status can prove to be disruptive to the established family order and lead to tensions between the woman and her main role senders.

State of Women in India by R. K. Tandon

Four months later, on a cool Friday afternoon, my Air India flight touched down at JFK. All the way over, in my Maharajah Class aisle seat, I had to pinch myself to believe that I had made it this far.

There had been a point, a few months ago, when my father had stopped being a chronically unreasonable and terminally conservative parent and had found his way into the land of acceptance. It had happened after a phone conversation with his brother Lal, who lived in Fort Lee, New Jersey – something about a fertile community of single young Indian men in those parts.

'Let her come, Gul,' Uncle Lal had said. 'Unworry. Vinita and I will take care of her. She can stay here. She can study and then also there are plenty chances for her to meet good boys, hah?'

Moderately convinced and only slightly comforted, my parents released their hold over me. I filled in some forms and was accepted into a School of Continuing and Professional Studies at New York University, which I thought sounded very grand.

There, I had decided to take courses in contemporary world studies, and current business and marketing trends.

'Look, Ma,' I had yelled out in delight when the brochures finally arrived. 'They even have a cafeteria just for international students. Just for us!'

I would be beginning my studies a semester late, but I had earned enough credits as an employee of my father's company, listing 'visual merchandising and image management' as my experience on the NYU application form. I played down the family connection, and the school's registrar, for that matter, didn't bring it up either. With a student visa brightly inked into my passport, and a suitcase full of winter clothes that I had flown to Delhi to buy, I was on my way.

Still, it had been the scandal of the community, and I felt as vilified as if I had pole-danced naked at a funeral. And even though my parents had agreed in principle to send me, my mother's face was morose, racked with shame.

'I know, I know, what can I do?' she tut-tutted one evening to Aunt Jyoti as I packed. 'Girls these days. You can't control them any more.'

My aunt, of course, was no help at all.

'You know how much people will talk, Leela,' she said. 'Girls who go to Umrica become too free, too spoilt. Then they can't adjust. Then no boys want them. You should have more control over her. At least here, you can watch her. But there? How are you to know what she will be getting up to over there?'

My parents had made one quick trip to the US several years ago and never went back. They had spent most of their time in Fort Lee, with the exception of the dutiful visits to the Empire State Building and the Statue of Liberty. Thus, their view of America – its culture, its people – had been shaped mainly by their weekly doses of *Dynasty*. ('No shame,' my mother would lament, as she watched Fallon week after week sleeping with everyone. 'See, even with her driver she's misbehaving. *Besharam!* Anju, don't watch this! Go to your room!')

Seeing as Uncle Lal and Auntie Vinita were unable to make it to the airport that day, Anand had arranged for a friend of his to pick me up. I knew my brother's friend as soon as I saw him – he had the look of a newly free Indian male, once destined to take over the family business back in Delhi but now revelling in the cultural lawlessness of America.

'I hear your parents kinda freaked out,' said Vijay, taking my luggage trolley. 'Hey, my parents woulda freaked out too if my sis was doing this.' The accent made me smile – neither Indian nor American, neither here nor there. Just like Vijay himself.

'They were OK at the end,' I answered. 'But I know

129

they still don't like it. It's OK for the boys, nah? But for girls, it becomes *such* a drama.'

'Well,' said Vijay, loading his Saab with my luggage. 'Your bro gave me the background. If you think it was hard to find a husband before this, by the time you get back there, babe, you're toast.'

As we drove, Vijay talked of his New York life as a final-year student at Fordham. Interesting as it was, I was profoundly jet-lagged and I struggled to keep my eyes open. Eventually I succumbed to sleep. When I woke up, I discovered to my huge embarrassment that I had drooled all over my jacket. We had also just pulled up at my new, temporary home.

It was quiet here, suburban, green, clean. Each house on the street had its own driveway, its own garden. Some lawns were cluttered with toys and tricycles, others held barbecue grills and deckchairs. It was the America I had seen on some of those television shows, the kind where big white men in baseball caps drank beer and laughed at one another's jokes while their blonde wives in nice dresses made potato salad in the kitchen.

'Very good, you're here,' Uncle Lal announced, greeting us at the door and giving me a hearty slap on the back. 'Umrica will be a most good experience for you!'

I had always liked my dad's younger brother. He was a cheery sort of man, never prone to dark moods or sadness. It was as if he took the very essence of optimism and injected it into his veins every day.

Auntie Vinita, however, was another story. She and my mother, sisters-in-law though they might be, never really got along. She was difficult, unsmiling, her temper easily provoked. The family reckoned that it was probably because she had never had any children. Now, she offered me a welcome as warm as yesterday's oatmeal. Her alabaster-white, heavily rouged face looked weary and worn; if she'd smiled, her make-up might have flaked off and fluttered to the floor.

I knew she was ruing the fact that she now had something else to deal with, and that she considered it insane that, at my supposedly marriageable age, I was cavorting off to college.

Vijay unloaded the luggage, and helped cart everything indoors, out of the cold winds that were beginning to gather.

'Come, sit, you must be so tired!' my uncle said, pushing me down onto the far end of a flower-patterned sofa. Vijay stood in the foyer, looking lost.

'Gotta get back to the city,' he said to us. 'Good to meet ya both. Anju, take care, need anything, gimme a call. You got all my numbers, right?'

I nodded, uttered a meek thank you, and watched Vijay go, dreading being alone with my relatives. Then I turned to look at them, seated on the couch opposite me. The room smelled of vanilla pot-pourri, and it felt warm and pudgy like my uncle. On a green marble-topped table in front of me were plates piled with cookies, and a pot of cardamom-rich tea. For a second, I felt at home. I helped myself to a snack and a cup of *chai*, and sunk back into the sofa. It was only five in the evening, but it had already turned dusky outside. Apart from the sullen breaths I heard emanating from Vinita's nostrils, all was quiet.

I suddenly felt forlorn. This had been a fun adventure – the plane ride over and meeting Vijay and listening to his stories. But now, all I wanted to do was to turn around and go home.

'*Kao, kao*,' my uncle said, pushing a platter of Danish butter cookies towards me. 'Or maybe something else? A sandvich? Co-cah Co-lah?'

I thought it interesting that my brother's friend could be here for three years and now be speaking like a semi-American, while my uncle and aunt, in this country for thirty years, still had the accents and lingo of people who had just stepped off a boat from Ahmedabad. I wondered what I would be talking like by the time I left, a year from now.

'I hear you're a great help to your dad in the shop,' my uncle said jovially. 'You can help me here too, right? Of course, only if you have time, away from your studies and all. Same business, family business, all that!'

I nodded and smiled, too tired to respond.

'Why don't you go upstairs and rest?' my aunt suggested, speaking for virtually the first time since I'd arrived here. 'I'll show you where is your room.'

I stood, and followed her up the pink-carpeted stairs,

132

down a corridor lined with white doors with gleaming brass handles, until we arrived at one at the far end.

Two hours later, I awoke, startled. It was dark, and for a few long seconds I couldn't remember where I was. It was only the smell of pot-pourri, which had pervaded the entire house, that reminded me.

I got out of bed, switched on the lamp next to me, and took a good look around. Everything was frilly, flowery and pink. Framed paintings of garden and river scenes, pretty yet bland, hung on the embossed wallpaper. There was just the small, single bed that I had been lying on, a chest of drawers, a dressing table and a tiny stool covered in rose-printed fabric that fell to the carpeted floor. It was the room of a simple teenage girl. Which, in many respects, I still was.

I discovered the bathroom next door, and washed my face. Then I went downstairs, almost tiptoeing, as if I were trespassing. I followed the sound of the television – that comforting, rhythmic Hindi *filmi* music that had greeted me virtually every morning of my life, and that I'd heard seeping underneath the closed door of my Bombay bedroom long after I went to bed.

'Come, come, did you rest well? Join us,' my uncle said, jumping up when he saw me. He and my aunt had been sharing a packet of Frito-Lays and a tub of cream cheese and chive dip, biding their time until dinner.

'Hungry?' he asked, as my aunt kept her eyes focused on the television screen. There, a buxom black-haired maiden wailed when told that her police chief husband, the love of her life, had been killed in a car crash. I had seen this film. He's actually *not* dead, I wanted to cry out! There *is* a happy ending!

'Hah, I'm feeling a little hungry,' I replied. 'But no rush, whenever food is ready.'

'Next Sunday, there's a function in the temple nearby here,' my uncle informed me, making conversation while my aunt scooped up the last of the dip, relishing the misery she saw on the screen in front of her. 'We'll go there, to the function. There will be a lunch there. Plenty young people from around here will come. You can make friends, nah? Maybe after, you would like to go to a mall. Have you seen a mall, *beti*? Plenty plenty shops are there, you can buy anything. Then we will have pizza and come home.'

'That's fine, Uncle. As you wish.'

After a homemade dinner of *puri* and *channa masala* and more small talk, during which all three of us diplo-matically avoided talk of my matrimonial issues, I offered to do the dishes and clean up while my relatives settled back in front of the television to watch the rest of the film.

'I've seen it already,' I said, when my uncle suggested that I join them. 'And I'm still tired, so I think I'll go upstairs and read a little before sleeping.'

Then, as I was about to mount the stairs, I turned to

them and said: 'Thank you for everything. I am only here because of you.'

A flicker of tenderness appeared on my aunt's face, tiny emotion-filled crevices lining the thick pink powder. I felt a little reassured then, less of a burden. A calm descended over me, telling me that everything would somehow turn out all right.

On the first day of college, my uncle drove me in his blue Volvo all the way to 70 Washington Square South, going considerably out of his way from his showroom-office on Broadway. On the way, he pointed out the bus-stop near home, the Port Authority, the various subway stations here and there, cautioning me to watch for the ones that said 'Uptown Only'. I nodded, taking it all in, scared, excited, confused, like a child going to school alone for the first time should be.

I gazed at a subway map my uncle handed over from his glove compartment, gasping at the sight of all those tiny, multi-coloured veins running across the large, folded page. Lettering I could barely read, numbers sprinkled across the creases. I would never learn my way around, and wondered how all these people did it, rushing and crossing streets and leaping out of taxis and pulling out of driveways.

I was wearing jeans and a red sweater; small black boots covered my feet. As I descended from the car, the cool morning winds took a good-natured swipe at my face, and a novel sensation overcame me. I turned my back on my uncle in his car, my new brown leather satchel swinging from my shoulder, and walked up towards the entrance of this imposing brownstone, its flagpoles brandishing blue and white banners, and that feeling intensified.

As alone as I was in that moment, I felt like I finally belonged somewhere.

As I knew I would be, I was the oldest person in all my classes. And I lied when I spoke to my parents later that week, telling them that I had made many friends very quickly. Apart from my interactions with teachers, I'd said very little during the course of most days. For lunch every day, I took a small tub of yogurt and a sandwich and sat on a stone bench on the campus grounds, reading. There was no tiffin-boy to bring me hot okra curry and soft *rotis*, no driver to take me home, no Indu to compare diamonds with.

But I watched as the other students coupled or grouped up, noticing how it was always the blonde girls who stayed together here, the dark-haired ones who gathered there. There were girls and boys together too, and they always seemed to be laughing at something, leaving me feeling as if they were perhaps laughing at me. Each time I felt as if I should be making more of an effort – 'just go up and say hi'. I beat down the impulse, telling myself there was no point, I would be going home soon, this was just temporary. But often, one or two of the dark-haired girls would throw over a look of quizzical recognition. They were from India too, or perhaps Sri Lanka, or Pakistan, or Bangladesh. Third world, in any case, and sub-continental, all of them wondering silently what I was doing here. They were all younger – nineteen compared to my twenty-six. Girls just starting out, choosing an education before the inevitable early marriage; not, like myself, someone who came to college because they needed to escape the fact that they had failed at the most basic task of finding a mate. On occasion, I would glance up at the chattering girls, and then turn back to my book.

But one Wednesday afternoon, between a class in prose-writing and an introduction to contemporary media studies, I made my first college friend.

'You dropped this,' said a voice behind me, as I walked down a corridor. I turned and saw one of the dewy, dimpled, dark-haired girls smiling at me, holding out a folder which I had accidentally let slide to the floor.

'Oh, hah, thank you so much.' I deposited the file back into my satchel.

'My name is Devika,' said the girl, still smiling. 'What's yours?'

'Anju,' I said, and forced myself to continue the conversation. 'Um, is this your first year?'

'Third, actually. About to graduate soon. And you?'

'Just started. I'm doing a professional course. Got my

bachelor's in Bombay already. I'm just doing a year here, then going back.'

'Great,' said Devika, in that unmistakable Indo-American accent. 'We should have a coffee sometime. I know it can be hard, being new.'

'Hah, it's OK. But yes, I don't mind a coffee. Maybe after my next class?'

We met at Starbucks a couple of hours later, where I was horrified to learn I had to pay more than three dollars – around a hundred and fifty rupees – for a cup of coffee. In India, that would buy two friends and me a full-scale *dosa* lunch.

As we both fiddled with Sweet 'n' Low packets, the inevitable question hung in the warm, aromatic air between us.

'So, not married?' Devika asked, a question I had been anticipating.

'No, not yet. You?'

'No, still studying. Perhaps when I return to Delhi. Soon, I hope.'

She was twenty-two, pretty, thoughtful, polite, still with that lilting, lingering accent that defined her as a Delhi-ite. She was lean and long-haired, with skin that smelt of Lux soap. A tiny diamond glinted right above her right nostril – so ethnic, yet somehow it worked with the black shirt she wore close to her body, tucked into black jeans. She was a business management major, and, like myself, had been allowed to come to school provided she

138

stayed with relatives – in her case a married cousin who lived on the Upper West Side. It was also easier for her, she told me, because both her parents were 'educated'. Her father was a judge in Delhi, her mother a teacher.

'They both believe in polishing the mind, although they would have preferred me to do that closer to home instead of flying here,' she said. After her first year, her parents relented – perhaps also because she had outstayed her welcome with the cousin – and allowed her to get campus housing.

'But no sharing with boys,' Devika said, mocking her mother's stern directive.

'At least you are nearby to the school,' I said, enjoying the conversation, not quite realizing until now how much I'd missed it. 'Me, I stay with my uncle and aunt in Fort Lee. So I can't really do anything after school. You know how it is.'

Devika nodded, recalling her year with her well-intentioned cousin, when all her own comings and goings had been closely monitored. She'd had to be home by ten on weeknights, a curfew that extended to midnight on Fridays and Saturdays, but even so, Devika always needed to let her cousin know exactly where she was, who she was with and where she could be reached. It was a situation that reflected my own. It wasn't a hugely jarring thing for either one of us, given that parental surveillance had been what our lives had always been about anyway. But here, in the context of the freedom of our hip new experiences, the strings that bound me to my relatives seemed weirdly out of place. Mostly, I was just embarrassed about it. I could have been off at museums and art shows or even just sitting in one of the many cafés that surrounded the college – or, like most students, doing the clubs at night. But it simply wasn't worth it. Such was the litany of questions thrown at me by my uncle and aunt – Where? With whom? How late? How are you getting there? – it was often easier just to stay home and watch *LA Law*. It wasn't as if I had lots of friends yet anyway. And the fasting – I was still doing Monday, Thursday, Friday – made socializing inconvenient at the best of times.

But in Devika, I felt like I had found a consort, a confidante, someone who just got it without me having to explain everything.

'Come to MOMA with me tomorrow,' Devika said brightly, finishing the last of her coffee. 'There's an exhibition I really want to see on women painters, and some Indian artists are included. If your class schedules allow it, maybe we can go together.'

Thus began my first New York college friendship, one I was happy to share with my uncle and aunt. Devika was one of our own, a misplaced, mildly disgraced girl from India, here for a snatch of freedom and fun before finally donning a gilt-embroidered red sari.

*   *   *

'I need to tell you something,' Devika said to me one Saturday a few weeks later. We'd lunched in town with my relatives, and then the two of us rumbled off on the subway to Times Square to see *Cats*.

'What?'

'I'm seeing someone. You know, like dating.'

I gasped, my face a picture of shocked naivety. I hadn't seen Devika as a dating sort of girl. Why, just the other day, she'd been talking about her parents having lined up some prospects in Delhi for her. But maybe Devika would have a 'love marriage'. That would be interesting, and as long as her parents liked the boy, it would be a good thing.

'But listen,' Devika continued. 'Nobody knows. Not my cousin, nobody.' She paused. 'He's not Indian. He's American.'

I blinked, imagining Devika's light chocolate-skinned hand entwined with that of a white boy. That's what my mother and father and uncle and aunt called them – white boys. My wool trousers made me slide around on the plastic subway seat, my sweaty hand clasped onto the metal pole next to me for support.

I didn't want to hear this.

'Oh, God.' I was astonished but tried not to show it. This was precisely what people back home feared – that their young maidens would come to the US, find an American male to be with, and never return.

'I'm really in love with him,' said Devika, raising her voice to be heard above the screeches of the train. 'He's

141

a sweetheart.' Her face fell. 'But I don't know what I'm going to do. I have to go back to Delhi and he's known that from the beginning but now that it's just a matter of a couple of months, it's really hard for me. I just want you to know because I feel as if I can't talk to anyone else here. My American friends don't understand it, they think I should just stay on here, get a job, or maybe take him back to India and introduce him to my family. I mean, it's really that serious between us.'

'Why are you telling me?' I asked. 'I don't want to know about all this.'

No doubt, Devika had been like me once – devoted to her culture, overflowing with piety for her parents, committed to returning to India as virtuous as she was when she had left. But now she was betraying all of that, and I almost felt tainted by association. She was giving the rest of us girls a bad name.

'Because sometimes I might need you to cover for me,' Devika pleaded. 'Like when Rob and I go away for weekends, I can tell my cousin I'm with you. You know?'

I gasped again. Not only was my new friend going out with a white boy, she was obviously in some sinful arrangement with him, just like on *Dynasty*.

'I'm not comfortable telling lies for you. But don't worry, I won't tell anyone your little secret,' I said, a meanness in my voice. I ended the conversation by turning my attention towards my fingernails.

We sat through *Cats* in silence. And, although Devika and I often passed one another in the halls of NYU, we never talked much after that. Even though I had been the one to initiate the end of our friendship, it hurt. I missed her. But I needed to keep my distance. The last thing I wanted to do was become like her.

I was never allowed to lose sight of the real reason I was in America. Everyone else thought it had something to do with 'broadening horizons', or other such noble endeavours that I might read about in that *Ms* magazine distributed on campus. But it was no such thing really. Not for me, anyway.

'Any boys?' my mother asked, during one of the twice-weekly trunk calls from Bombay.

'Not really, ma,' I replied, sadly. 'But don't worry, we're trying. We're going to a party today, and Uncle Lal says a boy from Chicago will be there.' Each time we spoke, it was important for me to proffer some morsel of hope.

Later that day, I accompanied my uncle and aunt to the Swaminathan Center, a religious-cum-social retreat located on a quiet side street not far from their home.

This was a monthly gathering. I had been once before and had felt so out of place among the young mothers with irritating husbands and cranky children, and teenage girls hiding from their parents what they had done the night before, the boys they had kissed and the beers they had guzzled down. I'd had such a crummy, lonely time, I vowed never to return.

But I'd had little choice today. My uncle had made mention of a suitable boy, the son of his friend's cousin or some such convoluted relation. The prospect in question was also the owner of a men's clothing store in Chicago – a respectable business.

'There are the parents of the boy,' my uncle said surreptitiously, as if he were offering me a line of cocaine.

I looked over at a small, squat couple eating from the buffet table as they made their way along it.

'The boy is not here today, but the parents will meet you and you can see a photo of him. If you like, we pursue, hah?' he said, reasonably. 'Here, come, come, let's go say hello.' He put his hand on my back, and gently herded me towards the crowded buffet table.

'Hello, *bhau*, so good to see you again, welcome to New *Yawk*, or shall I say, New Jersey! Hah! This is my niece, the one I told you about.'

Mr and Mrs Squat remained expressionless but took me in, head to barefoot toe. The mother had the most serious overbite I had ever seen on a woman, so I hoped the son had had better luck orthodontically. The father's white shirt had yellowing sweat stains under the arms; his too-tight trousers were pulled up close to his chest. He needs to go shopping at his son's store, I thought, then considered, horrified, the possibility he already had.

But I smiled, casting my eyes downward, and saying a quick, 'Hello, Auntie, hello, Uncle, how are you?' before allowing my uncle to make generic small talk. Not very discreetly, the mother took out an old airmail envelope from her black patent leather handbag and handed it over.

'The boy's photo,' said my uncle, leading me back across the hall. 'We'll look at it later.'

On the way home, I pulled the colour print out of its wrapping and smiled. He seemed to be about my age, photographed standing behind a counter lined with shirts. There was no animation in his face, knowing as he did that the image served its purpose without any need for embellishment. White shirt, black pants, hands clasped behind his back. Small round glasses, a tuft of a moustache, hair parted down the centre and combed flat.

And slung around his neck, like a noose, was a measuring tape.

'Let's see,' my uncle and aunt said in unison, as we stopped at a traffic light.

'Looks nice,' he said, nodding at the photo.

'But why the measuring tape?' said my aunt, giving voice to my own question.

'Why, nothing wrong,' Uncle Lal said.

'Yah, but it's like a scientist sending a picture of himself holding a test tube.' I interjected. 'It just seems a bit try-hard, no? And really, I don't think I waited this long

145

to end up marrying a tailor who can't even dress his own father properly.'

I simply wasn't interested, for a whole bag of reasons.

But the biggest one was that, by then, I had met Jeff.

Chapter Nine

But for the Indian woman a foreign marriage is seldom a positive act; it is, more usually, an act of despair or confusion. It leads to castelessness, the loss of community, the loss of a place in the world; and few Indians are equipped to cope with that.

India: a Wounded Civilization by V. S. Naipaul

He had been at Starbucks one afternoon. I saw him just as I finished reading the *New York Post*.

'Are you done with that?' he asked, as I turned over the last page of the tabloid, and rubbed the black stains left behind on my fingers onto a paper napkin. 'It's inky, isn't it?' He smiled.

I nodded that yes, it was, and, of course, he could by all means take it. The cappuccino machine whirred and whooshed behind the counter. I inhaled deeply of the hot milk and brown sugar, cinnamon and coffee beans – I came here as much for the warming smells as I did for the beverages.

He was dressed in a suit, but had loosened the silver-grey silk tie around his neck. His eyes were the same colour as his shirt – a cornflower blue – his hair dark, his face angular. At first sight, he reminded me of Adam Carrington: lean, upright, classically good looking. But he smiled, and there was an openness in his face that made me feel that it was OK for me to be sitting alone here in a coffee bar, *kind of* talking to a white man. The first white man I had spoken to off-campus, not counting the guy from whom I bought subway tokens.

'Um, yah, have the paper,' I said, glancing at my watch but not really paying attention to where the hands were. 'Hah, OK, bye.'

'Gosh, you're from India, huh? But really from India . . . you still got your accent and everything.'

'Yeah, uh huh, have to go, OK, um, bye.'

And sweeping up my things, I was gone.

He started coming to Starbucks every day at two in the afternoon, about the same time I went in there for my daily fix. There were more polite smiles and nods and newspaper-exchanges – I took his *USA Today*, he took my *New York Post*. After a week of this, we started sharing a table.

He just wanted to chat. So he and I swapped brief swatches of information: he was from Florida, came to college in New York and stayed. He worked as an advertising executive in a big, trendy, downtown agency. He loved what he did, wooing clients and getting them to commit to his company. He was good at that, he said to me smiling. Oh my God, was he flirting?

After another week, he asked me to lunch.

'That is, if you don't have class. Or maybe dinner would be better?' he asked.

I had never been asked out before. I had never even seen it happen on television. There, people just seemed to end up kissing, or in bed, or married. But there was never any lunch.

'Um, yah, thanks, but it's a bit difficult,' I stammered. 'I do have classes most days, and in the night I go home quite early because I'm staying with my uncle and auntie in New Jersey, you know, and they get worried if I come home late, so thank you but I'd better not.

'And also,' I continued nervously, unbidden, 'you know, it's not such a good idea, because my parents don't want me to become too friendly with the people here. We're quite a conservative family and they don't want me to have all these undue influences from the West. You're very nice and all, but I cannot at all conceive of undertaking anything more social with you, I hope you understand.'

'I was thinking about a sandwich,' he said, still smiling. 'Not eloping.'

We finally had the sandwich, a late lunch on a Saturday at Balthazar.

'Food,' he said, when our orders arrived. 'Isn't it nice to have a conversation over food instead of paper coffee cups?'

Jeff wanted to know all about me. Did I love college? What was it like living quietly with relatives in the suburbs while the city was bursting with things to do? If my parents were so conservative, what was I doing here in the US anyway? What did I do when I wasn't in college? Wow, and what was India like?

And I loved being able to talk without having to watch my words. In between bites of a wholewheat with mozzarella, eggplant and pesto – thank God today was a non-fasting day – I could tell him what my American life was really like. He didn't know my last name, didn't know my parents, didn't have my phone number. I was a random Indian girl he'd met over a double latte. In a few months, my course would be over and I'd go back to Bombay, feeling all the richer for experiences just like this one.

'I feel lonely, mostly,' I said to him. 'I mean, I'm really enjoying my class work. I'm so glad I came here to do it. But when classes are finished, I go home and so my spare time is spent mainly in New Jersey. I read about the things happening here in the city and I hear people at school talking about this show and that show, and I wouldn't mind being invited along. But my uncle and auntie really don't like it when I go out. They want to know who I'm with and how and when I'm coming home. It's too problematic, so I don't do it. So it's lonely.'

'Don't you think your parents would like you to really benefit from your time in New York, seeing as they've invested so much in you being here?'

'That's a most American view of things. Of course not. They let me come only after I cried and begged and told them how bored and unhappy I was in Bombay, that I needed to get out. And the conditions were that I'd stay in New Jersey, behave properly, and let uncle and auntie search for a good boy for me.'

Jeff looked puzzled.

'To marry,' I added. 'While I'm here, they're trying to get me married.'

'Wow, I'd heard about this kind of thing still going on,' he said. 'I think there was a documentary on PBS about it. But how do you feel about it? You don't seem like the kinda girl who'd go for an arranged marriage.'

'Why? Because I don't wear my hair in braids or speak like I just got off the plane from Bangladesh? You know, it's a tradition. It's something we've been doing for thousands of years, and it seems to me that it works. I barely even know anyone who's divorced. Can you say that? I'm not saying that everyone who goes in for an arranged marriage is happy. But they stay, because their expectations are different. In America – like they show on TV – it's all about wanting everything all the time. Never just being content. You know what I mean?'

Jeff just raised his eyebrows.

'And anyway, it's not so different from what you people do here, this dating thing. For us also, it's like dating. But the date is chosen by our family, and the main difference is that we have to decide right afterwards if we want to marry the person or not. That's all.'

'But that must put so much pressure on two people

meeting for the first time,' said Jeff, obviously intrigued. 'I can't even imagine wanting to marry any of the girls I've been out with.'

'Then why did you go out with them?'

'Well, they were nice enough. You know, we all need to be social, we need to interact with people of the opposite sex. We find people attractive, and we take them out and explore that attraction. Most of the time, it doesn't work out, but that doesn't mean we should stay home for the rest of our lives.'

He paused.

'So, um, you've never had a boyfriend?' he asked, tentatively.

'No. I've never even gone on one of those what-you-call dates. So far, I've only talked to boys that my parents have approved of, and even then, I've never gone out with anyone alone. If a guy is interested in me, he must tell his parents, who will call my parents, and we'll see each other that way.'

Jeff was a keen, wide-eyed listener, a man hearing this for the first time, utterly disbelieving, muttering something about 'Practically in the twenty-first century – how can this happen?' But there was a part of him that was enchanted by the way I had it all mapped out, imprinted on my psyche. It seemed folkloric in a way; sacred.

'What about love?' he asked quietly, moving closer to me. 'Don't you just want to fall madly in love?'

154

An old Julio Iglesias song was playing in the background, the rain had just started to come down outside, and the restaurant was growing still and quiet. I had begun to feel a soft stirring inside me, a longing and loneliness. For just a fraction of a second, I wanted to touch his hand, which lay inches away from my own. It was clean and white and with just a sprinkling of dark hair on its lean fingers. I had never touched a man's hand before, not even my father's.

'Love itself is magnificent, but if people think that's what they feel for someone when they start dating, they're wrong,' I said. 'That's why they get divorced, because what they thought was love was something else. We don't even have a term for "falling in love" in our language. Instead, we say *pyar hogaya* – love has happened. That's what it's about. You see someone's kindness, their suitability for you, your heart opens to them, and love then happens. And when all your families are around to bless you and support the union – there is no greater magic than that.'

How I yearned to be chosen by a fair-skinned Indian man dressed in a white silk tunic. How I dreamt of his parents coming to mine, their arms outstretched, asking for me, saying they would take me 'in a sari' – Indian-speak for 'without a dowry'. How I knew that being selected by a stunningly eligible man – the kind that all the girls wanted – would finally win me the approval I had never had.

So it was easy for me to be disdainful of anything else. I told Jeff, in the most critical terms, how I had watched over and over as my classmates eased into these things called relationships. The young, bright students around me never seemed not to be in one. In little clusters in the hallway, they would talk about someone they met or 'made out with'. They talked of spending weekends and going on vacations and it seemed to me as if they regarded this whole matter of dating and relating as if they were deciding what to wear every morning. Discretion and careful long-term choices were not part of the moral mix. Still rooted in my uptight, desperately upright Indian culture, I found that to be baffling.

Lunch turned into dinner (I had told my uncle and aunt that I was at a student event) and we had a nice time even though I had to be home by eleven. He told me there was something 'unattainable' about me, which made me smile, given that my parents were happy to toss me towards just about anyone who would have me. I let him have his delusions. He told me he loved the gleam in my black hair, the brown patina of my skin, the lilt in my accent. I had never been appreciated in such a way, so I warmed to him even more.

Then there was another dinner a few days later, and another after that. On our third dinner date, at an Italian place called Nino's, he touched my hand as we waited for our platters of pasta primavera. I let him, because I needed him to do it. We had time to spare before my

156

curfew kicked in, so we went to a comedy club. There, the spotlight was on someone else. Jeff and I had a table in the back.

He picked up his mug of beer and drank from it, then turned to me as I laughed at the female comic's jokes about her obsession with her answering machine. He put his arm around my shoulders, and pulled me in closer to him. I turned to face him, and as I did, he placed his lips on mine. I was startled, but it felt nice, so I let him do that as well. The closest I had come to being kissed was when I had pressed my lips up against my bathroom mirror to see what I might look like. Fish-faced and bug-eyed, I wasn't appealing. But Jeff had his eyes closed, while mine stayed open. It was over in a few seconds, and I had another sip of my Shirley Temple while he went back to his beer.

And so, while a wild-haired American woman stood beneath a hot light and told funny stories about PMS and shaving her legs, I was ushered into my first romantic relationship.

I still wanted to be the long-haired Hindu wife. But until then, this would do.

I began to chastise myself for the way I had treated Devika, who no doubt by now was back in Delhi, missing Rob, probably soon to be wed to someone her parents had found for her.

I had read in *Cosmopolitan* that dating should be fun, flirty, exciting. Most of the time I just felt torn and confused, distressed at the inevitable chaos I was causing to my karma.

But I consoled myself with the fact that, in a few months, I would be heading back home. Jeff and I both knew this, but it was never discussed. Between now and then, if anybody found out that I had been cavorting with a white man, I would be shipped back to Sahar International Airport in Bombay before anyone could say 'interracial marriage'. For I never, even remotely, entertained this becoming anything more than what it was: a 'casual relationship'. I shuddered when I thought of it, that I was basically no different than all those light-skinned girls at college who held hands with one boy one week, and another the next. The difference being, of course, was that apart from a few kisses on the lips, Jeff wasn't going to get any further. I was saving myself for my Indian prince and for the wedding night I had always dreamt of, when I would slip into a peach silk negligee with a matching gown, and he would hold me from behind as I gazed out the window and up at the full moon, and then he would lead me to our rose-petal strewn bed.

I'd obviously read one too many Harlequins.

To have that man be Jeff was unthinkable. Already, I could hear my mother's voice in my head: 'Are you crazy? What are you doing? Who is he? Why do you want to spoil your reputation?'

In addition to being on a short leash, it wasn't as if I had plenty of friends I could entrust to 'cover' for me, so seeing Jeff was always a complex and wearying experience. As far as anyone else knew, I was attending a seminar, working extra hours in the library, anything that would keep me out of the house for a few hours here and there. He was never allowed to call me at home. And when I called him, our conversations were brief, stagnant, impersonal. There was always someone around or the television was on, with its incessant images of young Indian damsels running through meadows, pursued by hairy-chested studs in tight white trousers.

The core of Jeff's life was freedom and adventure. The core of mine was restraint and caution. On top of that, I was guilty and afraid all the time. There was no way this was going to work.

Sure enough, less than three months from our rainy-day lunch at Balthazar, the end came. It was a balmy summer evening, when Uncle Lal and Auntie Vinita thought I was attending a film class. Jeff and I decided to dine at Ignacio's, a lively Cuban restaurant mid-town he'd been keen to take me to. He went off to park and I went inside, where I saw my aunt's best friend and her family being seated. If she saw me with Jeff, the news would blaze back to my Fort Lee relatives before the dessert plates were cleared.

Instinctively, I turned and hurried back out of the restaurant. Jeff approached, his car keys jangling in his pocket, holding his hands up questioningly. 'We can't stay,' I said quickly. 'My aunt's really good friend is in there. I'm not supposed to be here.'

'Enough of this already,' Jeff said, standing back, colder and angrier than I'd ever seen him. 'This is stupid. Enough. We're going to go in there, and we're going to have a nice dinner, and not care about who is inside and what they think. Got it?'

'Jeff, no.' A compression of sadness was forming in the back of my throat. I was afraid, equally scared to be caught lying but also of losing this sweet-natured brown-haired blue-eyed boy I had come to really like. I knew that I was being forced to choose between being with him, or pulling up my petticoats and sprinting off. 'I'm not going back in there. It's not worth the risk to me. There are a hundred other restaurants around here.'

'So, basically, I'm not worth it to you, is that what you're telling me? Is that what it comes down to?'

'I'm leaving soon, Jeff. What is the point of upsetting everyone so you and I can have Cuban food? Let's just go somewhere else. Please.' I started crying. Please, God, don't let him leave me. I started chanting one of my many mantras: '*Om broom bruhas pataye namaha. Om broom bruhas pataye namaha.*' Please, God, make him hug me and say it's OK, and we'll go to around the block to the Italian place instead.

He didn't. He turned around towards his car and strode off.

For a moment, I stood on the pavement and cried.

I wanted to phone someone, to tell them what had happened, to hear a sympathetic voice. But I had no one to call.

So instead I hailed a taxi, went to Grand Central, boarded the NJ Transit, and headed back home, claiming to my uncle and aunt, who were surprised to see me return so early, that a migraine had prevented me from seeing the rest of the film. In bed that night, I hid my head under the soft pink cotton pillow and wept for a long time.

And when there was nothing left, I told myself it was for the best anyway. Karma and all that. I had owed Jeff something from a previous life, and I had just repaid it.

When I awoke the next morning, I slipped back into my student's clothes again, took my own coffee in a Thermos from the kitchen, and headed off to college. I told myself Jeff had been a whimsical adventure. I wasn't going to let it get to me.

But the experience had had its effect, none the less.

'I don't want to come home, Dad,' I said to my father one Sunday. The *dishoom-dishoom* of two villains battling played out on the television in front of me. 'I'm happy here, and don't want to leave yet. My school counsellor says I can stay here a year and work, that it's part of the student experience. I'll be earning and everything. It won't be hard to get a job. Please, Daddy?'

'Anju, that's craziness!' he shouted down the phone line. 'Over my dead body will you stay in Umrica. We had an arrangement – one year of school for you, then

161

enough. Then back here. You haven't even bothered to find a boy. What have you been doing there?'

'I graduated, Dad. I did really well. That's why the counsellor thinks I should stay here.'

'Your counsellor knows nothing. You have a return ticket. You will use it. You are coming home as planned.'

'Daddy. Please. I haven't had much time to meet anyone, being at school and all. But now, I'll have more time. I'll be able to meet more people through Uncle Lal and Auntie Vinita. They've been trying so hard, but I've been so preoccupied. I promise, just give me one more year, and I know I'll find someone. You know, Dad, I need an educated boy now, and I won't find anyone like that in Bombay. Please.'

There was a sigh of exasperation on the other end of the phone.

'*Beti*, what are we going to do with you?'

My father sounded hurt and disappointed, but I steeled myself against his entreaties, to the way in which he tried to make me feel guilty. If there was one thing I had learned from my year here, it was that I wasn't ready yet to return to Bombay. If I got back on that plane, as my father had wanted, I would be returning to a life that would be so much less lived than the one I could have if I stayed here. I would be going back to a dreariness comprised of married couples, their kids and critical, interfering relatives. Maybe I was becoming bitter. But New York was the place to be bitter in.

'Even Anand has returned here from college and is working with me,' my father continued. 'So now both your brothers are here. Why must *you* stay away? You're the girl. Daughters are supposed to stay home until they marry. Finish.'

'Please, Dad, it's just another year. Maybe less. Please.'

A week later, I found a job with That's A Wrap!, a small publicity and events company in the downtown section of Madison Avenue, where I was one of only seven employees.

By mutual agreement, I had moved out of my uncle's house in Fort Lee. Aunt Vinita was quite happy to see me go, evidently tired of being my guardian. Uncle Lal owned a small studio on the Upper West Side, which he let me have at his 'family rate', which, despite its value, still gobbled up more than half of my weekly salary. But I rode the subway, ate cheaply, and lived the life of any other twenty-something just starting out in this strange, wild city, while thousands of miles away my parents fretted and fussed and fumed.

Sometimes, I wished I still had Jeff. With no uncle and aunt to placate, my life was finally – more or less – my own. But he hadn't called me since the day he walked away from me on Sixty-Fourth Street. And I was simply too unsure of myself – what I wanted, who I was – to call him. Besides, what had really changed? I may have been living on my own – something that I knew my parents had taken great pains to hide from their friends – but the shadow of familial responsibility still hovered over me. Even if I were to see Jeff again, I would have the same problems – fear of being seen, the shame of openly dating a white man, guilt at having abused my parents' trust. I just couldn't do it.

'Why don't you have a boyfriend?' asked Kris, a funny and friendly accessories editor I had met at a hand-bag launch, and whom I was treating to lunch. With her curly blonde hair and happy face, she reminded me of Kyra Sedgwick. In Bombay, they hadn't even heard of Kyra Sedgwick. Gosh, I was really in the inner circle now.

'How to do?' I swivelled my wrist and spread my fingers in that way that only Indians could manage. 'From where will I find a nice Indian fellow?'

I let it become my trademark, this endless, ongoing, pervasive search for a mate. My new friends thought it was quaint. One of them tried to fix me up with the guy who ran her neighbourhood 7-11 ('What? He's the right colour, isn't he?'). When I declined, she told me I should hang around Lexington and Twenty-Fifth, where all the *masala* vendors and sari shops were.

'You know, Kris,' I tried to explain, 'nobody in my family has married outside the community. Nobody. Ever. In fact, they have almost all had arranged marriages. Even in the case where one or two of my cousins met their spouses on their own, they always asked for the blessings of their parents.'

'There's got to be a first,' Kris said. 'You meet lots of great guys, don't you? What about the owner of Jazz, that boutique you're representing? Now he's a dish – Italian, hot, sizzling.'

'I tried the white boy thing, Kris. Last year. It just didn't work. I was always scared of being caught. Tell me, how many men are going to put up with someone who won't hold their hand in public, for fear of being seen?'

From nowhere, I felt tears come on.

'Honey,' said Kris, putting her hand on mine. 'Get emotional about it, weep all you want. But do it at my therapist's office. You haven't been here long, but trust me, you're going to need a therapist. It's like the Prada knapsack. Everyone just has to have one.'

My parents would have fainted. It cost a hundred dollars an hour – 4,500 rupees – which was what my father's general manager earned last month. The minutes were ticking into my assigned time, and I was still waiting in an outside office, its walls sponge-painted a cool mint green, the space filled with tan leather-and-chrome furniture. Even the magazines were hot off the press. Whatever was I doing here? Had I been abused? Abandoned? Molested? Was my dad an alcoholic, or my mother a cocaine-addict? Didn't people who go to therapists have *real* problems?

165

A door leading to an inside office opened, and out came Comtesse Véronique, whom I recognized from the pages of *W*. She was dabbing away at her eyes while trying to keep her mascara intact.

'Dhaarlink, tank you so verrrhy much,' said the Comtesse, who must have been at least 112, but had been slapped into shape by some Beverly Hills surgeon. She only *looked* seventy-six. 'Same time tomorrrrrhow,' she announced as she swept out of the office, a floor-length sable trailing her.

'Sorry to keep you waiting,' said Lorraine Vinas, New York's most sought-after therapist. I had imagined that she would be homely, maternal, perhaps sporting an old perm and dressed in cheesecloth and sandals. Instead, I was faced with a sculpted figure terrifying in Thierry Mugler and retro-style glasses, her black hair wrapped into a chignon. 'Come on in,' she said, unsmiling. 'Something to drink? Water? Please take a seat right over there.' She pointed to the end of a black leather sofa and gently eased herself into a big chair, across from me. Under her intense scrutiny I felt dwarfed, which was irritating given that my every intention was to appear happy and sane and together – so much so that she would say to me that I had no need of her services. I wanted to graduate before the first lesson.

A super-sized box of Kleenex sat on the glass table between us. Otherwise, the office was almost spartan apart from an imposing crystal statue of a naked woman in one corner.

'Wow, that's something,' I said.

'Yes, I commissioned it especially. It's me,' Lorraine replied, beaming.

'Excellent.' I forced a nod and a smile. The words 'manic vanity' pinged around in my brain.

'Right, to business. What can I do for you?'

'Um, well, my friend Kris, I guess she comes to see you, well, she said you could maybe help me, I mean, not that I have any huge problems or anything, but sometimes I get a bit confused, you know, not really knowing who I am and all that, but I guess that everyone gets that from time to time, so I really don't see what the big deal is, but anyway, here I am.'

'OK, take a deep breath now,' said Lorraine, lifting her notepad. 'What was your name again?'

'Anju. A.N.J.U. Anju.'

'OK, Anju . . . pretty name . . . take a deep breath, you seem all riled up. Everything is fine, we're just going to talk, OK, just talk. And keep breathing. Tell me a bit about yourself.'

'Well, I'm kind of living here in New York against the wishes of my parents. They want me to go back to India so they can find me a husband. Marriage is very very important to us, you know. We have to do it, and at an early age. I feel like I'm letting them down. But even though Bombay is my home, I don't feel like I fit in there any more. All the girls I grew up with are married. Most of them even have kids. I have nothing in common with them. So I was hanging around the house, working a bit for my dad, but mostly feeling like a burden. Like every time my parents looked at me, they saw their own failure. So I came here, although they hate that. And now I get lonely here, as I haven't really met anyone, and the guys I do meet are, you know, white, and I don't want that either. I'm scared of that.'

Lorraine had her fingers interlocked beneath her chin, her elbows resting on her notepad.

'Right,' she said. 'Here's my preliminary reading of the situation. You're from a third world country, trying to adjust to life in America. It's a big change. Your family has a pretty fixed idea of the way you should be doing things, and you're not doing them that way. So you're feeling conflicted, confused and guilty.

'Well, here's the truth, dear. This is *your* life. They can take it or leave it. You're your own woman. You're, what . . .' she said, glancing down at her notepad. 'Twenty-seven? Right, at that age, women in America have their own lives. You're a woman in America now. Get over it, get on with it.'

'Um, yeah, but it's not as easy as that.' I felt those tears again, but resisted reaching out for a Kleenex. 'I really love my parents. I don't want to hurt them. I don't want to let them down.'

'There's no such thing as win-win in situations like these,' Lorraine pronounced. 'I've seen lots of cases like yours, the heiress who wants to marry the parking lot attendant and is moaning that her parents are pissed. Of *course* they're pissed. But, like I said to her, what do *you* want? You wanna live in some walk-up in Brooklyn, go ahead, but just don't run crying to Mommy and Daddy when he expects you to take out the trash.'

'So what did she do?' I asked, much more interested in that story than I was in my own.

'She dumped his ass, of course. In the end, she decided she didn't want to marry poor. I knew she just wanted to get back at her folks, wanted to terrorize them. Are you sure there's none of that in you?'

'Um, I don't think so,' I replied, thoughtfully. 'They're really good people. They just have certain expectations. That's all.'

'Then they're not so great,' said Lorraine, in a voice filled with more bitterness than that shown by the sum total of all the Park Avenue matrons who came in here every day. What was I doing here, in this strange woman's office, justifying my parents?

'It's time to cut the cord,' Lorraine continued. 'Time to say *adiós*, see ya, *au revoir*. Time for you to get on with your own life. Is that something you find hard to do?'

Now I couldn't help but to reach in front of me for a tissue as I softly started to cry. Lorraine stood up, as stern as ever, her own feelings compressed into a tight, tiny bundle.

'Come here, we're going to try something,' she said. She

held out a hooked index finger, and asked me to curve my finger around it. 'Now, I'm going to pull your finger towards mine, and I want you to yell "no". Got it? Don't let me pull it. Just yell "no" as loud as you can. Right, I'm starting.'

Lorraine began to pull my digit, linked on her own, towards her.

'Come on!' She raised her voice. 'Say no! I'm pulling your finger away. Say no!'

I complied, not really caring where my finger ended up. 'No. No, no no. No,' I said weakly. 'Um, can we sit down again now, please?'

Lorraine straightened herself, looked down on me, and pronounced her diagnosis.

'You have issues with assertiveness. You feel you must be submissive in order to be loved. We have a lot of work to do. Our time is up now, but I'll expect to see you at least twice a week, every week, until we've resolved some of these negative messages you give yourself. OK?'

'Um, fine. I'll call.' But I knew that I wouldn't. I would rather be my messed-up but well-meaning self than the terrifying – and obviously single – tyrant who had just taken my money, a woman as cold as the crystal replica of her that stood alone in the corner.

But at least I had learnt to fight for my finger, if it ever came to that.

Chapter Ten

Women must be honoured and adorned by their fathers, brothers, husbands and brothers-in-law who desire great good fortune. Where women, verily, are honoured, there the gods rejoice; where, however, they are not honoured, there all sacred rites prove fruitless. Where the female relations live in grief – that family soon perishes completely; where, however, they do not suffer from any grievance – that family always prospers. Her father protects her in childhood, her husband protects her in youth, her sons protect her in old age – a woman does not deserve independence.

Sources of Indian Tradition,
Volume 1, edited by W. M. Theodore de Bary

One year, two months and three days after my departure from Bombay to New York, I returned home.

'It's just for a visit,' I told Marion, Milo and the girls. 'I really need to go back and see my family, make sure they're OK with what I'm doing here.'

'What if they don't let you leave again?' Erin asked, absent-mindedly shuffling some papers on her desk. 'What if they, you know, tie you to the bed or something? Marry you off against your will? It happens you know; I've read the books.'

'Don't be so dramatic, Erin. I don't belong to a Saudi sheikdom, for God's sake. My parents aren't barbarians. I'll go visit for a month, and then come back. You'll see.'

The sole male employee, Milo, was a tall, skinny red-head from London, who virtually lived in tattered Levi's jackets that he insisted on calling 'vintage'. When I had first started working, he had described my Bombay-to-New York transition as 'not so much culture shock, baby, as culture electrocution.' He wasn't far wrong, either.

In the weeks leading up to my trip back, I had to deal with all the necessities: finding someone to water my plants and pick up my post, making sure all my press releases were in perfect order, checking in with my clients to let them know they would be taken care of for the next few weeks by someone else in the office.

But, even more crucially, I had to do everything I could to return to Bombay a visibly changed woman. Confident. Clear-skinned. Happy. Beautiful. Like the kind of girl you might see in a Clinique ad.

I needed to be living proof that breaking away can be good for you.

'See yourself walking down a flight of crystal stairs,' the dulcet voice implored on my latest visualization tape. 'Be your dream.'

'Every step you take is as light as air, yet sure-footed. And with every step you take' – my concentration would typically be impeded at this point as I imagined Sting singing in the background – 'see yourself become more and more the woman you want to be. You are grounded. You are love. You are radiant. You are your own woman. You are you.'

It was all very Helen Reddy, but I subjected myself to fifteen minutes of this every morning before heading out to an aerobics class. I had also stepped up my beauty regimen, reintroducing the stinging lemon-doused chickpea-flour mask my mother used to slather on my face as a little girl. I *had* to return to Bombay at least two shades fairer.

Then there was the wardrobe. I would be seeing everyone for the first time in more than a year: Indu, and all those other people I used to hang out with before they sidled off into coupledom. I wanted to walk into the dinner parties held in honour of my return and have everyone turn and gaze and be astonished at my poise, grace and equilibrium – not to mention how fabulously shrink-wrapped I looked in my red Hervé Léger dress. Not that I had a red Hervé Léger, but that wasn't the point. I recalled having read in last month's *Cosmopolitan* that looking great was the best revenge. Revenge for what, I hadn't quite figured out yet. For being single still? For being the one left behind? Whose fault was that? And why did I want to punish everyone else for it by making them feel as if their lives were dull and insipid?

But there it was, lurking grimly in my otherwise good-natured soul, the little part of me that wanted to get back at all of them.

Yes, I would show myself to be the independent one, the successful, happy, living-for-herself one. The one not constricted by rules and husbands and mean mothers-in-law.

'*Beti*,' my mother said to me on the telephone the night before I was scheduled to leave New York. 'Thank the

175

Lord that you are coming back home. Fly safely, and we'll see you at the airport. And hide your jewellery. You know what Indian customs officers are like.'

The marble Ganesh felt especially hard and cold, its carved feet a little dustier than I had remembered. But this time, I remembered to touch them lightly, and then looked up again at my parents as they waited for me on the other side of the long hallway.

'Come, *beti*, you must be tired,' my mother said, settling me onto the couch next to her. She was being uncommonly warm.

It was suddenly quiet. No television, no phones, no Aunt Jyoti.

'So,' she announced, looking at me with a questioning eye. She said nothing, but I could read her thoughts as clearly as if they were scrawled across the night sky in flashing neon lights: *She looks different, thinner. Not eating properly. I have read how all these Umricans do this and that diet. But fairer, which is good. Maybe she has been using Promise of Fairness. Maybe you can buy it in Umrica. But she definitely looks smarter. Fancy fancy clothes. When did platform shoes come back into fashion? Small top, thin trousers. And her hair, cut in some layered style. And what are those beads around her neck? Doesn't she have enough real jewellery that she has to wear some fake rubbish? And where is the coral ring that is supposed to bring her a husband, and the black thread we gave her to wear around her left ankle to protect her from the Evil Eye, and the yellow sapphire to calm her nerves? My daughter looks so different. More than one year in Umrica, and I don't recognize her. Oh God, please let her not have lost her virginity.*

But my mother somehow stopped herself from verbalizing all this. Instead, she just said 'So', and sat quietly on the sofa.

I waited. I had been home exactly sixty seconds. I counted. Sixty-one. Sixty-two. Sixty-three. Sixty-four. Sixty-five.

And then it came.

'So? No boys?'

I sighed, smiled, looked over at my father and Anil and Anand who were also sitting quietly, looking, not knowing what to make of me.

'No mum, no boys.'

'But, *beti*' – my mother's voice grew frustrated, sharper – '*what* have you been doing there all this time? *What*? Lal and Vinita have been trying for you, no? You've been going to parties and meeting other Indians, no? So *what*? Beti, what?'

It was, of course, inevitable. I had primed myself for the questions, the result of my parents' inbred, firmly rooted concern for my lifelong happiness. During the twenty-hour plane journey over, I had had it all rehearsed: how well I had been doing, how happy, how busy. How my boss had been so pleased with my work that she had helped me get a work visa, and a green card was now under way. A green card! Mummy, Daddy, do you know how many Indian people dream of having a green card! And those lovely friends I had, Sheryl and Erin and Kris.

And of course I often saw Uncle Lal and Aunt Vinita, went to the temple with them one Sunday a month, and at least every few months went to the India Association of New York luncheon. And see, I had become friends with Auntie Sati's niece, who was married and living in New Jersey, and had talked on the phone with Uncle Pawan's partner, who was in Long Island. My friends in Bombay had given me phone numbers of the people they knew in New York and the surrounding vicinity and I had dutifully and obligingly called them all.

I had told my parents all this during my twice-weekly phone calls with them from New York. And now, sitting with them for the first time in all these months, in our familiar burgundy-and-cream living room, cooled and silenced from the world outside by the air-conditioner, now I could tell them all of it in person, so they could see the shine in my eyes, the glow in my cheeks. Surely they'd rejoice at the transformation from the shy and sad girl I'd been when I left to the radiant and self-assured one that had returned.

But my parents of course saw none of this. At least,

they were thinking, their daughter had not returned to them pregnant and drug-addled or married to some long-haired white guitar-player named Abe. For this, they were grateful. But I was still single.

'Cool. Reese's Pieces,' said Anand, pulling out the crinkly orange packet from my tote-bag. I had gone to town at the 99-Cents store, filling an entire suitcase with cheap Snickers bars and now-crushed cardboard boxes of sugary, hydrogenated cookies. They loved all this stuff here. I had also brought back all the other Bombay must-have staples expected from someone who was, like me, an 'Umrica-return'. Kraft cheese. Tang orange powder drink. Johnson's Baby Shampoo. Colgate anything. Dream products that signified wealth and plenty and imported exotica.

For Nina and Namrata, there were pretty sorbet-coloured T-shirts, although I knew Aunt Jyoti discouraged Western garb. And for my aunt, dozens of foil-wrapped triangles of cream cheese and packets of salted crackers. For my other female relatives, those random aunts and cousins that made up my sprawling family, I'd brought small and big handbags, sandals and shoes, loose silk blouses and elastic-waisted polyester trousers, all bought on Seventh Avenue on those occasional days when they opened up the showrooms for the public. And at the discount drugstore on Thirty-Eighth and Lexington, I'd found containers of Revlon blusher, Maybelline eyeshadow,

Sally Hansen nail polish, all in popular colours of pink and orange and red. I had spent almost a month's salary on all the gifts, but I'd wanted to return bountiful and abundant.

'So, how's it all going?' Anand asked, his watery American accent growing ever more diluted by the day, now that he was back in Bombay. 'You like it there, hah?'

'Yeah, it's great,' I replied, my accent, conversely, taking on that American twang.

We were in my room, unpacking the goodies. I looked around and felt comforted by the fact that it was just as I had left it. A double bed covered with a lilac quilted silk spread. All the cupboards and cabinets painted white, with tiny brass knobs. A three-way mirror attached to the dressing-table, on which was laid out a mirrored tray, a beaded tissue box cover, a tiny silver bud vase. It was a room that had never said very much about the person in it, and that bore no imprimatur whatsoever of the young girl who had grown up in it, cried on its bed, stared at its walls in loneliness and longing, and used to dream of herself staring into the three-way mirror, one day, dressed in bridal pink.

It was still the room closest to the main entrance, as decreed by one of the many swamis and saints the family had consulted. Surely, they must have reasoned, if I felt like a guest here, I would be compelled to leave? I must be as close to the front door as possible, with one foot – metaphorically if not literally – almost outside it. As

180

it turned out, I *had* left; just not in the way all the soothsayers had predicted.

'Don't worry about Ma and Dad,' Anil said, looking at me sympathetically. 'They're just worried about you. You know how it is, people talk. You can't blame them. But you're here now, so just have a good time. It's great to have you back.'

I looked over at my two younger brothers and thanked God for them. In my entire extended family, they were the only two who never made me feel like some ugly thing growing more gruesome by the day.

'I'm holding you back, aren't I?' I said, sitting down heavily on the edge of the bed, and focusing my gaze on Anil. 'I know you're waiting for me. Maybe you shouldn't. I mean, I don't know how long it's going to take. Look, I'm almost twenty-eight now. Maybe you should just go for it, if you find someone.'

'He already has,' said Anand.

'Really?' I asked, surprised. 'Who? How come Mummy didn't say anything?'

'Oh, shut up, Anand,' Anil replied. 'There's nothing. Nothing has been decided yet.'

'Lavina,' Anand continued. 'You know, Auntie Renu's daughter. The pretty one.'

'Oh, right, Lavina,' I said quietly. 'Isn't she sixteen or something?'

'Twenty-one, actually,' Anil replied. 'I don't know. She's a nice girl and all, but no lightning, you know?

181

Mummy always says the same thing: *pyar hogaya*. The love will come. But I don't know. And really, I'm only twenty-three, it's just that as soon as Vikram got engaged to Mira, everyone has really been on my case.'

I knew what he meant. It was about three hours after Indu announced her engagement and the rest of us became a cluster of potential brides.

'Hey, go for it,' I said, cavalierly, not really wanting to face the implications. 'She's cute, right? And Mummy and Daddy like her and her family right?'

'I just think,' interjected Anand, speaking on behalf of his elder brother, 'that she's the only girl in that group of friends that looks natural, and not like a Bollywood starlet. You know the type, no? All bouncy bouncy, and hair that is highlighted brown, and those stupid coloured contact lenses, and totally fancy clothes. This one is simple and sweet. I think she'll be good for the family.'

I wanted to roll my eyes, but didn't. A year ago, I'd too thought that this was the ultimate.

'Here,' I said, tossing over a Tootsie Roll each at my brothers, summarily changing the subject. 'Have a *chota* snack before dinner.'

After more than a year of planning, the Vikram–Mira spectacle – the one that would also double as a wedding – was about to begin. The betrothal I'd witnessed just before leaving for the US would become a marriage, coincidentally while I was home for my visit. A year was an unusually long time to wait, but Vikram had to spend six months in Prague on a business deal, and Mira took that opportunity to compile the most fabulous trousseau a bride had ever had: lingerie from Paris, shoes from Milan, pretty dresses from New York and ethnic clothes culled from all over India – the designer duds from Delhi and Bombay, the mirrored blouses from Rajasthan, the embroidered hand-woven shawls from Kashmir.

My parents were thrilled that I was here, not just because I was away from the clutches of those dastardly Umricans, but because I would be around for the nuptials. It was going to be the biggest wedding Bombay had seen in quite a while. And because both Vikram and Mira's families were so well known, relatives and friends were flying in from everywhere: London, Hong Kong, Singapore, Barbados even.

My mother, having performed the requisite due-diligence, knew that the marriageable folk who were coming were all in their early and mid-twenties, too young for me. But she was nothing if not an optimist. At the very least, the wedding and all the parties around it would serve as a sparkling showcase for unmarried types like myself. She had bought several new ensembles for me, all the latest styles. And even she – who was genetically programmed to point out a single delinquent hair beneath my eyebrows – had to admit that I was looking quite good since I returned from New York.

Perhaps, she ruminated, if I had been this nice-looking years ago, I would be married by now.

There were several days' worth of parties to look forward to. It would be like an extended convention of sorts, a series of mixers and networking gatherings where people met one another, made contacts, and kept them in mind for future opportunities. My mother hoped that someone would see me, remember a single male thirty-something distant relative, and have an ah-hah moment. That was how these things worked.

The celebrations began a week before the wedding, igniting with the *misri*, the official engagement ceremony where the couple would exchange rings, and garland and feed one another with slivers of cake after a priest had performed a short ceremony. To outsiders, it could well appear to be the wedding itself, so high was the glamour quotient with the rich embroidered saris, heavy Indian jewellery, stone-studded handbags, bouffant hair and dark red lipstick sported by all the women there.

The bride-to-be entered the hotel ballroom where the ceremony was taking place, and the chatter among the three hundred or so guests stopped to accommodate the span of loveliness in her wake. She wore a pale lavender-coloured sari, made of French Chantilly lace (or so everyone said) and embellished with silver threads. It had been custom-made, like everything in Mira's overflowing trousseau, by one of India's top designers. The gossip was that Mira's parents had spent more on one sari than most people spent on a wedding. Her waist-length hair, usually left long and loose so everyone could appreciate its black, gleaming beauty, was today twisted into an elegant chignon, with Mira wisely resisting all efforts on the part of her hairdresser to sprinkle silver glitter onto her tresses. Her face looked flawless – just the right shade of fair, a matching lavender eyeshadow adorning her almost-black eyes, which were rimmed with liquid liner. A smidgen of rose-coloured blusher on her smiling, smooth cheeks; a perfectly appointed mouth framing teeth as straight and white as piano keys. Around her neck and on her ears she wore simple diamond platinum jewellery, but everyone knew that that was just for the entrance. Soon, Vikram's two sisters would decorate their *bhaujai* – literally, the one born for their brother – with a jewellery suite that those who had seen it said was magnificent.

'Can't be so great,' whispered my mother to her sister as talk of the baubles circulated the room. 'They didn't buy it from us.'

Mira exuded an air of frailty. Instinctually knowing how to play the part of the coveted, delicate bride, she sat down next to her intended on a throne-like chair atop a red-carpeted podium. All their immediate relatives and the priest stayed close at hand. Everyone else milled about in the main part of the hall, like members of the audience in an interactive stage show. Which was, essentially, what this was.

Vikram wore a white silk kurta pyjama, its buttons a dainty shade of lavender.

Good grief, I thought, they're going to be colour-coordinated throughout this wedding.

For my part, I figured I didn't look too bad – for a renegade – and was secretly grateful to my mother for the stash of new clothes. Today, I wore a lemon-yellow chiffon sari, with a sprinkling of beading, and pearl and citrine jewellery from my father's shop that I'd asked him to copy from a Bulgari ad. From a wrist that jangled with dozens of glass bangles also hung a ruched silk bag, in a go-with-anything shade of metallic beige that I'd fortuitously picked up at Daffy's for just such a purpose. On my feet, Blahnik knock-offs achieved the desired effect of giving me additional height and a streamlined silhouette.

'Hi, Anju, you came back,' said Indu, with a cold kiss on each cheek. I stepped back and looked at my one-time best friend, the girl I hadn't spoken to since I'd left.

Indu looked a little puffier and her eyes were more cloudy than I remembered. Still, she was beautiful in an emerald green sari, a complexion like gossamer, and a massive chunk of jade around her neck. Her obvious misery notwithstanding, Indu was still a fine-looking young woman.

'How are you?' I asked, lightly touching her hand. Compassion, I reminded myself. Sincerity. Non-judgement. I was learning about this at a course in Buddhist meditation

I had just started taking. About not letting my own personal angst get in the way of seeing someone else's.

'I'm fine, husband is good, the boys are good, and another on the way, see?' she said, smiling now, pointing to her expanded stomach.

'Congratulations, Indu, that's great news.' I smiled. How come nobody had said anything yet, about my own new relaxed, open and confident persona, about the hip new hairstyle and the toned new body and the great accessories? How come no one noticed?

'So, you look nice,' Indu said, as if reading my thoughts. 'Nice haircut. Did your mummy buy your sari for you from here?'

'Yes, I guess she wanted me to be prepared for all these functions,' I said laughing, hoping that I would be able to segue into a conversation about my fabulous and fun life in New York, the people I had met, the parties I had gone to, and yes, that time I had to seat John Travolta at a fashion show *personally*. Imagine!

But Indu didn't ask me about any of that, and nor did any of my other old friends. It was as if I had never been away at all. Good thing I didn't buy the red Hervé Léger dress. It didn't look, three days into my visit home, as if anyone was going to throw me a dinner party.

*   *   *

'*Beti*, so nice you're looking,' said Vikram's mother, smiling broadly to reveal teeth smeared with red lipstick. 'Are you enjoying yourself? Did you eat?'

'Yes, thank you, Auntie. Auntie, congratulations on Vikram's engagement. Everyone is so happy. Really, they are such a lovely couple. Mira is looking so pretty today. And that necklace is exquisite, Auntie.'

When talking to one of my mother's friends, I transformed myself into the pleasant, enchanting daughter, interested in everything pleasantly mundane about their lives – their maids, their jewellery, their grandchildren. All I really wanted to say was: 'Where's the bar?'

I glanced around the room, heaving with sari-clad women and their young daughters and daughters-in-law, and felt myself to be slightly above them all, what with my independent New York life and all. And because of that, I could afford to be generous with my compliments, even if I myself was not – for now, anyway – on the receiving end of any.

Immersed in her own inane banter on the other side of the room was Lavina, the lovely young girl who wanted to become my brother's wife. The Vikram–Mira nuptials had presented her with an ideal opportunity; given that Anil and Vikram were such good friends, as were Lavina and Mira, there would be plenty of occasions for all of them to meet. In addition, I could imagine that Lavina was relishing the thought of Anil seeing her at her loveliest, in those new saris and *gagara-choli*s her mother had bought for her, the heavy silks adorned with gold threads and the

188

light chiffons dusted with seed pearls, all dripping with youthful chic and selected because they promised to be the most alluring outfits in the room.

Lavina did look particularly pretty today, striking in an embroidered turquoise tunic, matching slim trousers and a rich shawl draped over one shoulder. She wore high, thick heels, bought from Metro in Colaba and the latest style, with the big rhinestones all over the front. She was sexy and glowing, safe in the knowledge that Anil wouldn't be able to resist her radiance.

'She's looking pretty hot today,' Anand said to Anil, as they spotted Lavina hugging Mira after the ceremony. 'Everyone knows she really likes you. I think you should go for it. I want a *bhaujai* too,' he said.

Anil nodded, looked away, and took another sip of canned orange juice, his spare hand plunged deep into the pocket of his dove-grey silk kurta. He knew everyone was looking at him as the next-in-line, the groom's best friend and *such* a good boy. Tall, too.

But he was concerned for me. He looked over and noticed me scanning the room awkwardly, self-consciously. Aunt Jyoti was with me, forcing a chunk of *misri* – rock sugar – into my mouth. Tradition dictated that the eating of this at such a joyous ceremony would guarantee one's own betrothal. 'Now finish it,' Jyoti instructed. 'Then it will be your turn next.'

'Auntie, I've been eating this since I was fifteen. I really don't think it works.'

My mother, next to us, was immersed in at least three conversations simultaneously with her friends. But unbeknownst to me, she was particularly interested in one. Her friend Gopi, who was somehow related to Vikram's mother, was telling how she had just heard about Raju, a suitable boy for me, flying in tonight for the wedding festivities.

'Who is he, this Raju?' my mother asked, pulling Gopi to one side.

'My brother-in-law's brother's cousin's son,' she replied, making as if it were all one big happy family, which, given the gelatinous structure of the global Sindhi network, it was. 'He's also related to Vikram's mother, and so am I, as you know,' said Gopi.

But my mother wasn't too interested in the interrelational logistic, she just wanted to hear more about Raju.

'How old is he, and where does he live, and is he tall?' she asked.

'He's thirty-two, thirty-three, now living in London. His mummy and daddy live in Delhi, but the boy is on his own over there, making money and all.

'I think,' Gopi continued, lowering her voice as if she were exposing some heinous secret, 'the boy could be most good for your girl, as he is also like that, you know, independent-type. Hah?'

'And he's coming when?' my mother asked, already excited, her mind soaring ahead to my own *misri*. How propitious this would be – that she hears of a prospective son-in-law at the engagement ceremony of her friend's son, and her daughter happens to have returned from Umrica! It's all meant to be!

She was informed that Raju was flying in tonight from London, and would stay for the week, at the very least. He was here to see his parents who were arriving from Delhi to attend this glittering wedding, but also to find a bride for their son. He worked as an accountant, he was five feet eight inches with medium complexion, and 'no bad habits'. Perfect.

My mother decided it would be best not to forewarn me of this latest prospect. This was going to be her newest strategy – simply to introduce me to any boy who seemed appropriate without filling my head with preconceptions or giving me a way to back out too early in the game. My mother had also dispensed with the preliminary background check that often preceded such possible alliances. She decided she would wait to see if Raju and I at least liked the look of one another before investigating him.

'No sense making a big hullaballoo and then they don't like each other,' she said to my father later that night, when we all returned home. 'Let's just wait until they meet, and we can pretend like it wasn't pre-arranged, nah?'

'Leela, do what you want,' said my father, by now trained not to get too excited by reports of yet another prospect. 'But before you do, don't you think you should at least find out a bit more about him? These boys in the West, away from their parents, you don't know what they're doing over there. Drinks and drugs and gambling and all, so many bad influences.'

'Nonsense!' my mother retaliated. 'He's from a good family, and see, he's known to Vikram's parents. So let Anju and him at least meet, and then we can find out what we need to. No sense in stopping anything before it starts.'

Chapter Eleven

My love, my true mate
Lost by the Fates
Found by the moon.
My love, my true mate
Come to me
Now, don't delay.
(*Repeat three times.*)
  'A Love Spell', *The Goddess in the Bedroom*
                    by Zsuzsanna E. Budapest

Another night, another dinner party. I had been back home for a week now and had grown more disenchanted by the day, my hours filled with enforced visits to the hair salon, sari shops, the homes of random relatives for tea and wedding-related parties every night.

I felt alienated from the people I had grown up with; understandable in that many of them were now couples with infant children and vast domestic responsibilities such as whether to hire a third maid or not. My female friends, especially Indu, looked at me in a way that I could not quite decipher, but which seemed to border on envy. I supposed that was a lot more palatable than pity. Their husbands thought it was enticing, one of their own living alone in big, bad New York City, where there were strippers on the streets and people drank vodka for breakfast. They wanted to talk to me about my life there but knew their wives wouldn't like it, so they kept their distance.

I missed Erin and Kris and Sheryl and the lunches with clients and the lipstick launches. Right before coming here, I had begun to help Marion organize fashion shows, which I loved because it gave me something I'd never even had a glimmer of before: power. All those fashion writers from magazines and newspapers calling and asking for another ticket, a better seat. I always tried to be helpful and kind, but couldn't help feeling a little smug as I listened to their entreaties. There, in that tiny seven-person office in a nondescript building, I actually was someone that people wanted to talk to.

Here, I was now an outsider. It would have been different if I had escaped, like so many of my friends had, the respectable way – through marriage. If I had gone off with a husband to some far-flung corner of the world, and then returned to visit family and friends, there would be parties galore in my honour, curious questions, gifts and kudos and celebrations. But because no girl had ever done *this* – gone off alone, living single – I was the defective piece in a jigsaw puzzle: try as I might, I just didn't fit in anywhere.

'Come, *beti*, don't dilly-dally.' I heard my mother's voice through the door.

'Coming, Ma, I'm just putting on my bindi.' I fidgeted with a tiny bit of purple felt with a rhinestone embedded in its centre. Finally I pressed it flat atop a precise pore between my eyebrows, crouching close to the three-way mirror.

I stood tall again, and checked everything was in place. My amethyst-coloured sari had been perfectly pleated and tucked by our maid, its *pallav* gracefully draped down my back. On each wrist, I had on a dozen identically matching glass bangles that sang a happy tune as I ran a brush through my hair, added on a touch more lipstick, spritzed on some perfume, and declared that, at last, I was ready to go.

'House party, hah!' spat out Aunt Jyoti, holding a glass of cold Tang. 'Both sides are so rich, you would think that they could afford to do this in a hotel or proper restaurant. Too much trouble, coming to a dinner at somebody's house. Never enough seats. Too crowded, too messy. Where shall we sit?'

I stood next to my aunt and looked around. For once, she was right. As spacious as this house was, there were far too many people crammed into it. Servants holding big doily-covered trays of oily fried snacks and bowls of green mint chutney had to push through the crowds in order to get to everyone. Disaster was imminent in each square foot, as women balanced glasses of Thumbs-Up – discreetly laced with rum – with small plates holding potato puffs topped with ketchup. (Ketchup never comes off beaded chiffon, no matter what you do.)

As always happened at these things, the women – and there must have been at least 120 of them – congregated on one side of the large living room, taking up most of the seating space. Their husbands stood or sat in smaller cliques, or were pressed close to the bar that stretched across half the room, downing tumblers-full of Black Label Scotch whisky with one hand, and cracking open spicy pistachios with the other. They were a tipsy, raucous ocean of open-necked printed shirts and shiny gold watches.

These were friends of my parents, the parents of my one-time friends, relatives of relatives of the couple soon-to-be-wed. I reached out for a tray and, when no one was looking, poured a quart of white wine into my soda. It was already after ten, dinner was nowhere close to being served, and I desperately wanted to go home. My brothers were in one of the younger-boy cliques, the stars of the show, a riot of happy laughter and back-slapping gin-drinking.

I couldn't go there.

My father was in a corner in quiet discussion with the owner of a rival jewellery firm, discussing the current demand for fancy-coloured diamonds, while my mother was engrossed in a conversation about a temple in Kerala that was supposed to reward visitors with the fulfilment of all their prayers.

I couldn't go there, either.

Only my aunt Jyoti seemed happy to stand with me, as she looked around to see who was wearing what. But I braced myself, for as good as I thought I looked, any moment now my aunt would make some remark about my still not-fair-enough complexion.

And that's when I saw him, my antennae picking up the sense of disconnection that he, like me, seemed to exude. His was a new face, and new faces were always noticed here.

But this new face had just arrived and had still to acclimatize to the wild and wilful socializing, the heaps of people merry-making all over the house.

I stood and watched as he did the rounds, being led by a sweet-faced woman who was probably his mother. Everyone seemed interested in meeting him, given that his novelty quotient was high. His mother led him around the little cliques proudly showing him off. 'Yes, he is doing very well there in London, an accountant, *nahin, beta*?' she said, glowing as she looked at him.

He played his part perfectly, reaching down to touch the feet of just about everyone he met that was over the age of fifty, reminding me of a wind-up toy.

'Who's that boy?' my aunt asked, catching him as he surfaced from one of his feet-touching exercises. 'I've not seen him before.'

'Which boy?' I replied, pretending I had been looking at a large enameled picture of Krishna that towered on the wall next to me.

'That boy,' my aunt continued, unfazed by my show of ignorance. She pointed a finger covered in orange chilli sauce. 'There, the one with the short short hair. Hah, maybe it's Simi's son. Simi is Vikram's aunt, his *maasi*. He must have come from foreign for the wedding. I don't think he's married. No, definitely not. I remember, now, Gopi telling me that Simi was getting most worried about him, I think living in England, and not finding a wife. Let me go find out,' said Jyoti, putting down her plate and wiping the sauce from her fingers.

'Find out what?' I asked.

'Who he is, how old he is, why he's come, what he does, if he's looking for a girl now, if he's ready,' said Jyoti, speaking to me as if I were an idiot, before waddling off to join the rest of the crowd.

I leant back against the low table I had been standing next to, and rolled my eyes. Why was it that a boy had to be ready and a girl just had to be available, the assumption being of course that a girl was ready from the time she was ten? Just like my grandmother.

But at least he looked interesting. There was something slightly subversive about him, with his short, spiky hair that had been stylishly gelled, compared to the conventional side- or middle-parted styles of all the other guys in the room. And he was dressed quite beautifully, in what looked like Hugo Boss, and polished wing-tip shoes.

Across the room, my mother and aunt found one another and were joined by Gopi. They were talking quietly but excitedly, like three con-artists about to pull the scam of the decade. I knew better, of course. They were talking about me, and him, and how they would conspire to bring the two of us together without being obvious about it.

I turned to put down my plate, and he was standing right in front of me.

'*Beti*, this is Vikram's cousin Raju,' said Gopi, appearing at my side from nowhere. 'He's come from London, is a very top-top accountant over there. Raju, this is the daughter of my very good friend. Now you two youngsters have some company, no?' She nodded so hard that the bulbous hairpiece affixed to the back of her head looked like it was going to tumble to the floor.

'We're not in kindergarten,' I wanted to say, but swallowed my words. Instead, I looked at Raju, who smiled and nodded at me. I did the same. And then silence. Two perfectly capable, articulate, confident people who couldn't think of a thing to say.

'Er, so, you been here long?' Raju began.

'At this party? Oh, maybe a couple of hours. You just arrived, did you?'

I could tell that Raju was trying to place my accent. Bombay, but not quite; he was clearly considering the various inflections as if he were ascertaining the precise components of an expensive Chardonnay. His was resoundingly British. London, actually. With his brown skin, it almost didn't fit, it was so extreme. I could imagine him, back in London, doing all those English-boy things: drinking beer in pubs, playing games in gardens, rowing boats in the summer and coming ashore for strawberries and scones.

'Yeah, just got here. Actually, only got in last night from London. Came all the way for Vikram's wedding.'

'That's nice of you,' I said, smiling still. I was conscious of my mother and aunt, who had been rejoined by Gopi, watching us from across the room, my mother especially nodding at me to goad me on, to be charming, to capture his heart.

'What about you?' Raju asked. 'Are you related to his Mira, or were you just unfortunate enough to be dragged along?'

I laughed. At least he had a sense of humour. He would obviously rather be somewhere else too, and was honest enough to say so.

'My parents are very good friends with both families and my brothers are close to Vikram. So I'm just here.'

'And what do you do then, when you're not at boring dinner parties?' he asked, taking a swig of Thumbs-Up that I knew was laced with something.

'I've been working with my father. He owns a jewellery company.' I said nothing about being a publicist in New York and the fact that I was due to return to my life there in a couple of weeks, soon after the wedding. My mother had told me to pretend as if I was here for keeps, as she obviously hoped I would be.

'Oh, that sounds like fun,' Raju replied, clearly not impressed by the fact that I supposedly toyed with diamonds all day. But he continued to stare at me, taking in the shyness that tried to hide in my eyes, my fidgeting fingers, my lips that quivered nervously. There, his gaze lingered for a while longer than made me comfortable. I had read somewhere once that the more intensely a man stared at a woman's mouth, the more desirous he was of her. It was enough to make me break out into a light, warm sweat.

From across the room, my mother smiled. One of the many seers she had consulted had told her that I would meet my husband in a temple, surrounded by mythological motifs. This wasn't a temple, but surely, with a flute-playing Lord Krishna looking down benevolently upon us, it must be close enough? (My mother, however, was prone to stretching the possibilities. One palmist had told her that I would meet the man of my life 'somewhere near water, like next to a waterfall'; my mother immediately suggested a trip to Niagara.)

'I've said hi to everyone,' Raju announced, finishing the last of his drink. 'Do you think it would be all right with your folks if we went off for a bite someplace else? Can't bear this much longer.'

After approximately forty-five minutes of consultations all round, long goodbyes, and sorting out the logistics of house-keys – I'd never had my own – Raju and I prepared to leave. My father looked nervous, but Jyoti put his mind to rest.

'Everybody says he's a good boy. Let them go out and

get to know each other. No point them staying here, so many people, they can't talk. She won't be home late.'

I went into the bedroom to reapply my lipstick, and found to my total horror that a sliver of green pea had been lodged between my two front teeth all along. No wonder Raju had stared at my mouth so much.

Chapter Twelve

So I sympathize with those who so fervently want to find, and keep, love. But it can be frustrating dealing with singles, for often I find them woefully ignorant in their expectations and behavior with regard to relationships. Brought up by the old rules and playing by the new, they want to be intimate with others before they understand what intimacy is, and before they've been intimate with themselves.

Keeping the Love you Find by Harville Hendrix, Ph.D

'Right, sorry, let's go,' I muttered to Raju, once I emerged from the bathroom, vegetable fragment successfully excavated.

'Where to?' he asked. 'The coffee shop at the Oberoi, or the one at the Taj?'

'The Oberoi is fine,' I replied, knowing options were limited. It was wedding season in Bombay and everything would be crowded anyway. Most likely, we would end up waiting for a table, shifting from foot to foot, looking around, glancing at the time, awkward silences between us as we anticipated a waiter coming to break the tension.

We got into Raju's waiting car, after finding the driver, who had been off at the other end of the carpark with the other drivers smoking *beedi*s. We asked him to take us to the five-star hotel that was the hangout of Indians who could afford seventy rupees for a glass of *lassi*, which sold at pavement stalls for about one-tenth of that.

Raju said he was glad to be out of that house, that dinner party, away from those people with the loud voices and penetrating stares and rude questions. One of his mother's friends had even asked him how much money he made.

'Thank heavens we escaped,' he said, letting out a deep breath. I felt as if I were in some parallel universe. This was highly irregular, that my parents had let me go off with some guy that I – like them – had just met. What was that about? Usually, there would have been at least half-a-dozen steps that had to be taken before getting to this point, this sort-of-kind-of date: there would have been a conversation between both families, then my parents would have met Raju first to ascertain if he was indeed suitable for me, then there would have been the background checks and possibly even the matching of the astrological birth charts.

But there had been none of that. Or none that I knew about. Perhaps my parents had kept the proceedings secret from me. Or maybe, more likely, they had just lowered their expectations, relaxed the restrictions. I was almost twenty-eight after all, so maybe in the end my mother reckoned that Raju had a pulse, a job, and all his limbs intact, so how bad could he be?

'Do you like being here, back in India?' I asked him as we coasted down Marine Drive.

'Yeah, it's all right. Here to see the family and all that. But I'm glad I'm not living here. Too bloody – forgive my language – oppressive. The heat, the crowds, the dirt, the cows on every bleeding – sorry, again – street corner. You have to ask yourself how a country can progress when they've got bullocks peeing and poohing everywhere, right? I went to live in London ten years ago and haven't been back since. And I hope it's another ten years before I have to come back again.'

I couldn't get over his accent. I had never before seen a brown-skinned boy try so hard to sound like a white-skinned one. No wonder the aunties and uncles didn't know what he was saying – his working-class London banter sounded like a foreign language.

'What about you? What's your story?' he asked. 'Do you want to stay here for ever?'

My reply was crucial. If I told him I was a true-blue Bombay girl, which I was, I may alienate him. But if I told him that I had been living in New York, and had every intention to return there, the result could be the same. Not that it really mattered: such was the nature of these matchmaking things that all would be revealed soon enough – if not by me, then by someone else.

Still, I wished I knew how to play the game, to do the coy 'Oh, wherever life takes me, that will be OK,' thing that boys liked to hear. I had to be fluid, flexible, flowery, and just a little flirtatious. We both knew why we were here: he was looking for a girl, and I was looking for a boy.

If this went well, we could be engaged in seventy-two hours.

'Actually, I've been living in New York for about a year, and am just back here for a visit,' I said.

'Really?' Raju sat back, suddenly interested. I was surprised he didn't know – obviously, his parents hadn't said much to him about me, and that was fine. This way, I could start with a clean slate, as opposed to one that had been left dusty and grimy by other people's suppositions of what my life was.

'What, on your own and everything?' he continued. 'That's a bit unusual, innit?'

'Yes, I guess you could say that. But I really wanted to continue my studies, and once I finished them I stayed on and started working. Right now, I'm a fashion publicist.'

In the week that I had been back, I had not yet uttered those words because nobody asked and nobody cared. Sitting here in the back of this car next to a man I didn't know an hour ago, I felt like I wasn't going to be misunderstood.

It didn't take that long to be seated after all. Once we both returned from the washrooms, a table had been located. Of course, it helped that Raju had given fifty rupees to the manager. Smooth.

The white tablecloth reflected brightly underneath the overhead lighting, which cast a shine on Raju's spiky gelled hair. He fidgeted with his moss-coloured silk tie as he looked over the menu, while I recalled the last time I had sat alone at a table with a man who was neither my brother, uncle or father. That had been Jeff, almost a year ago.

Both hungry, we opted to share some *navrattan korma*, a plate of *paneer kofta* and some *naan*.

'Wine?' Raju offered.

I was tempted, but opted for a coconut water instead. He may be the liberal sort, but even liberal types have their limits, and drinking on a first date would probably be testing it.

I told him this, and he laughed. That gently eased us onward, into the gradual verbal revelations that made up a memorable conversation. It was like we didn't need to discuss why we were here, and simply enjoyed the fact that we were.

I felt like I was talking to a male version of myself. His own discomfiture with the society we had both been born into helped, strangely, to make me comfortable. With him, right now, I didn't feel so alone in my alienation. Even among my new crop of friends in New York, I never really had all that much to say. Sometimes I thought that perhaps they saw my life as insipid, that someone who lived a life as untainted by vice as I did couldn't possibly have anything interesting to share. My colleague

Milo called me 'Ma Walton'. And while Jeff was most enthralled hearing about the restrictions that had marked my life – something that painted me as hard-to-get and therefore so much more attractive – ironically, it was those restrictions that devoured the relationship before it really had a chance to begin.

In my week here so far, I had only had the most inane conversations with people, keeping the focus on *their* lives, *their* children, *their* maids. I was afraid to sound excited and happy because my old friends would never understand it, so removed were these components in their own lives. I saw them as shallow, they saw me as defective and any attempt at real communication was doomed from the start.

So what a joy it was to talk to Raju like this, to tell him of the roller-skating in Central Park, and my occasional trips to the ballet, and how I had recently come to be invited to the openings of the new clubs, bars and restaurants in that rough, boisterous, glittering city. There was also the possibility, I told him, of my being sent to Paris next month to help out with a fashion show being organized by one of the company's clients. Paris! Indu had gone to Paris on her honeymoon, but I didn't know anybody else who had ever been there. And certainly not alone.

Not surprisingly, Raju loved his London life. He had plenty of friends, and after work often met them for a drink at his favourite pub. (I knew it! I could read him so well!) His parents came to visit him twice a year, and while he enjoyed having them there, he laughed as he told me that after a week or so, he couldn't wait for them to leave. He would let them sleep in his bed and he took the couch, leading me to think what a good and kind son he was.

'They like visiting me in London, especially in the summer,' he said, mopping up the remains of the *korma*. 'They love Hyde Park, so I take them there all the time. They also can't seem to get enough of Trafalgar Square, which is bizarre given that we have enough bleeding pigeons in India. I try and get some time off work but if I can't, they hop on the bus and go up and down Oxford Street. Then they buy groceries and come home and make me a bang-up Indian meal. Nice to come home to that, innit?'

That was my cue to glide into a conversation about how I was sure a man like him would have *plenty* of people willing to cook for him. It was time to flatter his ego, caress him with my words, woo him with my sweetness. It was late, our inhibitions were lowered, and it was OK to be vulnerable.

'I'm sure you could have anyone cook you a wonderful Indian dinner, every night if you'd like,' I said, tentatively. 'I'd like to be able to do that for someone some day.'

Raju placed his hand alongside mine, letting our fingers barely touch. He told me that he thought I was sweet, that he liked the shyness in my eyes, and as he said that

213

my shoulders relaxed and I felt a growing warmth in my belly and in the air between us. He said he liked the fact that even though my father owned a jewellery business, I wasn't wearing much of the shiny stuff myself, and we both laughed.

I told him that this was the nicest evening I'd had all week.

When the bill came, I prayed that Raju wouldn't suggest splitting it. I heard they sometimes did that in America, but we were in India now and here, the men took care of everything.

Plus, I had no cash on me.

He laid down a five-hundred-rupee note, stood up and stretched, and came round to my side of the table to help me out of my chair. How very gallant, I thought, smiling. Soon, people from the party would be filtering in here for coffee and ice-cream, so it was a fitting time to leave. I turned to take one last look outside the window at the dark sea with its tiny curlicues of white foam. Marine Drive was deserted now. We walked through the glass doors of the coffee shop, his hand resting on the small of my back. I imagined myself in a red and gold sari, my covered head bowed down respectfully, this boy next to me in a cream silk *shervani* looking like a prince, making our way to the petal-covered double bed I had seen so many times in the Oberoi's glossy wedding brochure.

I had accompanied numerous cousins and friends to their bridal suites after their weddings, where everyone made off-colour jokes and ordered up obscene amounts of food from room service.

The next bridal suite I was going to step into was going to be my own.

Chapter Thirteen

A white rose given to a young lady signifies that the gentleman giving it esteems her love of the purest and most spotless kind that can be found in the innocent hearts of the gentle creatures of his acquaintance.

A Garter Round the Bedpost –
Love Charms and Superstitions

The smell and sound of samosas sizzling in a pot of boiling oil woke me up the next morning. As I opened my eyes, and recalled the night before, I smiled. I had that cosy-in-love feeling. So this was what I had been missing.

It was close to eleven, and the activity in the house was in full force. My father tended to go in to work later and later these days, often not making it to his office until after lunch. He knew he didn't have to be in all that much these days. He had a capable staff and a trustworthy assistant, Ramji, who looked after the finances and the day-to-day running of the five shops. And Anil and Anand would soon be involved full-time in the business so, at last, at sixty, he would be able to semi-retire.

My father had always imagined retired men to be the kind who stayed at home in their plain white cotton kurta pyjamas, legs stretched out on an ottoman while they immersed themselves in the contents of the newspaper or napped, or took long lunches or walks around Marine Drive with other retired men. After four decades of hard work, he should be looking forward to that.

But he had decided a long time ago that he wouldn't retire until I was married. That he did not believe his role as a father was complete until the day he blessed me with a touch on my bowed head as I sat in front of the wedding fire. It was, as far as an Indian parent was concerned, the ultimate benediction, more valuable than an Ivy League education, far more precious than an inheritance.

So, for now, he pushed to the furthest recesses of his mind any notion about taking it easy and looked towards the job at hand. He had to sign off some renovations at the Colaba store, investigate further the possibility of opening a branch in Delhi and decide if he should be investing more in fancy-coloured diamonds.

'So, *beti*, did you have a good time last night? You came home quite late, no?' he asked while he fiddled with his belt buckle.

'Yes,' I replied, not quite knowing what to say next. My mother, hearing that I was up and about, breezed in from the bedroom where she had been choosing among her stash of saris for one to wear tonight.

'Ay, *beti*, so late you got up! Did you rest well?' She was beaming, as if she was in on some secret that I had yet to be privy to.

220

Without waiting for a response from me, she launched right into it.

'So, *beti*, did you like him?'

'Yes, Ma, I did.' I was smiling and blushing like a pre-pubescent after her first kiss. 'He's a very nice guy. Very funny and intelligent. I like him a lot.'

'Ay, wah wah,' my mother lauded, jubilant. 'At last, someone you like! At last! His mummy, Simi, she phoned me this morning. I think also he has liked you very much.

'Now what?' My mother turned her attention to my father, who was extricating the bottom of his trouser leg from his sock, where it habitually stuck. 'Shall we arrange an official meeting between the families? How to proceed? I'll call Jyoti, she knows these things,' my mother continued hurriedly, flapping off into the bed-room again.

My father, ever the cautious businessman, remained quiet.

'Well, *beti*, it's good that you like him, but we don't know too much about him yet. Let's proceed slowly. No need to rush these things. Let your mother get excited, but we must consider everything, hah?'

I nodded, but wasn't really paying that much attention. Before Raju had dropped me off last night, he'd invited me out to coffee this afternoon. He said it would be a much more sane way to get to know one another outside of the frenzied wedding parties. I agreed with him, but at

221

that point was so besotted with this slightly rebellious yet infinitely charming man that I think I would have agreed to anything.

I decided to make a *besan* paste to smear on my face – nothing like the lure of romance to make a woman pay more attention to her appearance – and retreated to my room. I heard my mother on the phone with her sister, telling her how I'd finally met someone I liked. Was the next step to consult the astrologer on compatibility, or to wait until an official proposal was forthcoming? 'Do you think they'll come and ask for her?' my mother queried. 'Oh, so wonderful that will be! That his parents, they are such good people, will come here and personally ask for my daughter!'

All this excitement after one date, I thought. The girls back home wouldn't believe it. They went out on one date and obsessed about whether he'd call. Here, some twelve hours after meeting Raju, my mother was wondering if she had enough gold coins in her home vault to send over to his family as part of an engagement gift.

I heard my father on the other line to his secretary, Parmeshwari.

'Please take dictation,' my father instructed. 'And please fax to my friend Jeevan in London. "Dear Jeevan. I trust this finds you and family in good health. I require some assistance from you. We are considering a particular boy for our daughter, for matrimonial purposes. His name is Raju Asrani, and he is the son of Bhagwan and Simi Asrani who presently live in Delhi. The boy, to my knowledge, is currently employed by an accounting firm in London. He lives alone there. We know nothing more about him. The boy is currently in Bombay. Please conduct the usual discreet inquiries and come back to me as soon as possible with a full report. Do let me know if anything required on this side. Sincerely, et cetera, et cetera." '

I rifled through the clothes in my closet and hated every-thing there. I wanted to look fashionable yet conservative, pretty yet not intimidating. I smiled as I recalled last night, the way he looked at me as he dropped me home. We had talked for four hours. That was more than the combined length of all the one-on-one conversations I'd had with men outside my family in my entire life. Not counting Jeff, of course.

There was a lot to be said for aligning myself with someone of similar caste and background. The way he understood why I didn't want to order a glass of wine, and we could both laugh about it. He knew why I kept looking at my watch, being mindful of how late it was, and how in this case it was OK to 'be seen' as we were in the process of doing something noble, of making an effort towards matrimony. Anybody else outside of our society would have scoffed, but Raju understood. The momentous pressures and enduring obligations of our community seemed somehow lightened when we could both silently share them.

For that alone, it was worth marrying an Indian man.

I finally opted for a pair of white linen trousers and a light cardigan in a shade of creamy orange. My mother, even more exuberantly, stood outside my bedroom door and trilled: '*Beti*, are you ready yet?'

'My mum and dad asked me about you today. What I thought of you,' Raju said as we settled in our chairs at Trattoria, the twenty-four-hour Italian restaurant just off the lobby of the President Hotel. For a city filled with young people on curfews, I thought, Bombay had an awful lot of round-the-clock eateries.

We both ordered cold coffee with ice-cream, and I was using my straw to bob the big snow-white scoop up and down in the cup. I smiled a coy smile, the smile of a bride-to-be. Just as I was leaving home, my mother had called Raju's mother and the two had talked casually about the Vikram–Mira wedding and the weather and where you could find the best Banarasi silks outside Benares. But I knew that both mothers were sizing up the situation, hoping to rescue two wayward young people from the evil clutches of the West and return them to their rightful culture. I had heard my mother say to Aunt Jyoti that if the afternoon went as well as the night before, she would ask for Raju's birth chart and then call in Udhay the astrologer to do a compatibility rating. Surely, he would agree to the union. And if he didn't, as these things always tend to go, he would be offered a shiny gold guinea and a new sari for his wife, at which point he would certainly see things in a positive light.

'What did you tell them?' I asked, a warmth rising from somewhere in my body. Between us on the table was a single white rose, tucked into a silver-plated bud vase. Raju delicately played with its petals as I anticipated his next words.

'I told them I thought you were really nice, and that I like talking to you,' Raju replied, matter-of-factly.

'Oh,' I said, slightly disappointed.

Shouldn't there be more? Like: 'She's the most interesting and wonderful and lovely girl I've ever met. I can't wait to start my life with her.'

But maybe Raju just had some difficulty expressing his true feelings. At least he was understated and not gushy. My father had always said that such things start slow, on a foundation of practicality and friendship. 'Not like champagne that is fizzy when first you open the bottle, and then becomes flat after one-two days,' my father liked to say.

'My parents asked me about you, too,' I offered. 'I told them I thought you were very kind, and charming and so good-hearted.' I hoped to captivate him with my vulnerability, honesty and absolute faith in him.

Raju pushed his chair back so it was balancing on the two back legs, and swung back and forth treacherously. I remembered the more restless boys in college doing that, and how many times the chair gave way and they ended up on the floor. Everyone laughed then. It wouldn't be so funny now, although it did seem to indicate that Raju was nervous, which endeared him to me further. After all these years, this was finally happening to *me*!

'So, what do you want to do then?' Raju asked, a slight frown appearing on his forehead. 'We both know why we're here. So instead of letting our parents interfere, why don't we decide what we want? You know what my life is like in London. Do you think you could live there?'

It was this close, and could be this easy. This was a proposal, an offer of marriage couched in practical terms. All I had to do was nod my head, and say yes, I'd love to live in London, and this would be a done deal. Then we would both return home to our respective sets of parents, who would speak with one another, and an engagement could be announced tonight at the party. And everyone would congratulate us and wish us well and offer us thousands of blessings. There would finally be the parties in my honour. And, of course, my parents would be filled with pride and delight, two emotions that would be usurped by the biggest one of all: relief.

The whole situation was lacking in romance, but arranged matches weren't about romance. At least Kenny G. was playing in the background.

I wanted my parents here. I wanted them to tell me it was OK, that Raju was a good guy, that I'd be happy for ever. But because they weren't here, I didn't know what to say. I also wanted him to tell me that he loved me, which almost never happens this early in arranged unions. But I'd lived in America, and there, people *did* say those words before rings were exchanged. I had a feeling that I loved Raju, and would happily have told him that if only he would say it first.

'You're going to the party tonight, right?' I asked him. 'Our parents will be there. Let's do it then.'

I don't think my father meant for me to see the fax. But it was on top of the newspaper, a mother-of-pearl coaster weighing it down so it wouldn't be swept away by the breeze from the ceiling fan.

Of course, I had to look at it.

Dear Gul,

I have done the needful. Raju Asrani, according to reports, doesn't socialize with Indians. He has his own way of doing things. I am told that he has had one English girlfriend for long time. They are seeming to be almost married. Please abandon proposal. Let me know if anything else required.

Sincerely,

Jeevan

My face suddenly went very hot, and, for a minute, I

think I stopped breathing. I felt as if I had just been given a resounding slap across the cheek.

I sat down on the couch, and reread the greyish, powdery paper in my hands. If the words typed across it were true, and Raju did have a long-term girlfriend, why was he talking to me about marriage? I quickly tried to recall the Paths to Detachment that were part of the course in Meditation for the Modern Age that I had just taken. The instructor had advised us all to think of any kind of loss as nothing more than the loss of a pencil or something else very small. Attachment to anything – an idea, a person, a dream – would only lead to sadness.

But I was a single girl seeking love; how could I *not* get attached?

My mother emerged from her room holding a sari that was being delivered to the maid for ironing. She stopped when she saw me holding the fax, and the look of disappointment on my face.

'Ay, *beti*, don't pay any attention to that,' she consoled. 'That Jeevan doesn't know anything. I'm sure it's all just gossip. You like that Raju, no? We'll find out properly everything. Promise. Now go and start getting ready.' She kissed the air, something she had always done to comfort me, the times when I fell over in the playground or didn't do particularly well in an exam. Or, like now, when she could tell that my heart was slowly breaking.

*   *   *

It was approaching nine in the evening, and we were almost ready to leave the house. The wedding was still two days away, but tonight would be one of the most lavish and significant of all Indian nuptial celebrations. The *sangeet*: a night of music and dancing and indulgence on every front, mostly in rich foods and Scotch sodas. At an hour when most people in the civilized world were half-way through dinner, we had yet to make it out of the door.

I was the first one ready for a change, most likely because I wasn't all that worried about how I looked. Nothing like the looming demise of romance to make a girl feel like she doesn't give a damn.

My parents were talking in their room, obviously unconcerned that I could hear everything that was being said. They were discussing the contents of that fax.

'What rubbish!' my mother said to my father. 'This girl could be anything. A friend, an office worker. You know how people gossip. And, *bas*, so what if he has had a girlfriend? He's a boy, no? He's living alone in England where there are plenty loose-type girls. But now, he has decided to marry and he has come to us. I'll be very angry if you let some stupid rumour like this stop the proceedings. Let us at least give him a chance to tell the truth.'

I peered in through the open door and watched my mother drape her sari; twice around, take the furthest corner and make the pleats, throw it over the shoulder, pleat the base and tuck it in. She adjusted the folds, pressed down the *pallav*, gently kicked the hem-line to

229

make sure the length was perfect. Then she checked her jewellery to ensure all the pieces were tightly and firmly affixed, lightly spritzed her hair with spray and dabbed a drop of perfume behind each ear. She turned to look at my father who was standing by the window, looking out, handsome in his silk kurta pyjama.

Even for all my conservative upbringing, I knew there was nothing wrong with a romance here and there. While we had never talked about it, I knew my brother had had his share of flings while in college. For a boy, that was a part of his 'American experience', as everyone around him jokingly referred to it. Hell, even *I* had succumbed to the dating temptations of the West.

So maybe this talk of Raju and a girlfriend was nothing more than ignorant conjecture. Maybe she was a former flame. Maybe Uncle Jeevan had got it all wrong. But we were now on our way to the party, and as we rode in the car in silence, I knew that by the end of the evening, I would know the truth. I just wasn't sure if I really wanted to.

Chapter Fourteen

A college boy, instead of adopting what the West would call an enlightened view, came to see his diploma as a sign of increased worth, enabling his parents to demand more dowry for him.

May You Be the Mother of a Hundred Sons
by Elisabeth Bumiller

Lush strands of white jasmine flowers were strung across the ceiling like a shag-pile carpet. When we walked in, hundreds of people were sitting cross-legged on thick mattresses covered with saffron-coloured silk, or reclining against burgundy satin bolsters. Turbaned waiters roamed in their midst, bearing shiny trays with tumblers of Scotch, glasses spilling red and white wine, vessels of sweet juices. Others held aloft long dishes bearing hefty finger-food: fried *paneer* cubes, spicy pieces of chicken on skewers, potato *tikki*s to be dipped in mint chutney.

On a raised podium in the front of the room sat the musical troupe that had been flown in from Delhi for tonight's event. Dilbagh Singh, with his trademark golden turban and streaks of henna painted onto his beard like a tiger's coat, was a cultural institution in this country. He had hit after hit and performed to sell-out audiences across India and wherever Indians lived. Even I knew what a coup it was to have landed him for this event; I would have to explain it to my friends in New York as the equivalent of having Luciano Pavarotti sing 'Ave Maria' at their weddings.

But the unabashed grandeur of this event would hardly make for any moments of intimacy with Raju. Where was he? My eyes began scanning the room, falling on the silk-covered back of many a male, but still no Raju in sight. Many of the men had gathered around one of the two bars situated at the far corners of this large, rectangular ballroom, the grandest in Bombay. Mirrors that stretched up to the ceiling reflected the glow from the massive crystal chandeliers, and allowed women to stop and preen before moving on to the next conversation. Overdone finery was everywhere, especially radiating from Vikram and Mira, who were again in colour-coordinated outfits and seemed to blend into one another in a fusion of yellow and gold, like clashing comets. Mira's neck was almost entirely covered, like a Masai tribeswoman, by rows and rows of small rose-cut diamonds set in gold. I recognized the piece: it had been specially commissioned from my father by Vikram's mother. It was one of the many suites of jewellery the groom's family had had made from various jewellers around town, but perhaps the most magnificent.

Even my mother, supported by Aunt Jyoti, had to concede that this was quite a night.

'They've really gone all out, nah?' Jyoti said. '*Booootiful!*

Aiie, but *such* a waste of money, better that they give it to charity than throw it away on a big party like this,' she added, allowing her lips to fold over a flaky spinach-filled puff pastry.

While the food intake of one guest here would feed a Somalian village for a week, nobody was really complaining. Dinner, to be laid out buffet-style in an adjacent room, wouldn't be served for at least another couple of hours. And the guests, many of them already very high-spirited as a result of the free-flowing Johnnie Walker (Blue Label, only the best, my father pointed out), were on the dance floor right in front of Dilbagh Singh's podium, doing the *bhangra* and letting themselves be carried away in the performer's rousingly ecstatic singing.

Although we had entered as a family, we had by now dispersed. Anand and Anil had gone off to find the guys, knowing that they would soon be dragged up to dance as part of Vikram's entourage.

'So? Where's Raju?' my mother asked me, while my father tried hard not to look anxious.

'I don't know, Mummy. I've been looking for him as well.'

'They must be sitting near Vikram's family, being so close relatives and all,' my mother continued, pulling me off in that general direction.

'Please, you women don't do anything,' my father cautioned. 'I will talk to the boy and his family myself.' He pulled himself up and straightened his shoulders, reminding me of a cowboy in an old Western poised to fight for the virtue of a beloved one. While my mother seemed completely motivated tonight, blind to any complications, I could at least count on my father to really look out for me.

Trying not to trip over the mattresses and cushions and the inebriated people reclining on them, we attempted to see past the swaying, clapping folk on the dance floor. Slowly, we made our way over to Dilbagh Singh's podium, where, sure enough, Vikram and Raju and their respective parents were seated, snapping their fingers in time to the music and summoning forth more glasses of Scotch and soda. Raju looked up, saw me and only half smiled. I suddenly felt as if I were crashing a party. Why he was suddenly being so cold? I couldn't understand it.

'Gul, velcome, velcome!' Vikram's father shouted, leaping up to greet us. 'Come and join us, no? Here, take a drink! You just arrived?'

Vikram and Raju, who had been sitting cross-legged on one of the silk-covered mattresses, also stood up, both of them leaning over to hug me lightly. Out of the corner of my eye, I caught my father bristling when he saw Raju's lips touch my cheek, as innocent as it was.

'Hello, Uncle,' Raju said, extending his hand to my father who took it, shook it and nodded hello. The temperature in here began to feel unbearable. By now, even Raju's parents had stood up to welcome us all, and I was conscious of everyone around us looking upon this small group, all smiles and handshakes, so obviously focused on a single boy and girl with matrimonial potential.

After a few moments of small talk – Nice party! Good crowd! Vunderful singer! – my father turned to Raju and his father and suggested they find a quiet place to converse. As the trio turned to walk off, Raju glanced over at me, but he didn't seem to have much of an expression on his face. If anything, he looked annoyed as opposed to reassuring. It was quite hurtful given that, just several hours ago, he'd practically proposed. Perhaps he was just nervous. He was, after all, being carted off by my father for a serious man-to-man talk.

I hadn't spoken to Sheryl, but I had made up my mind.

If all that talk about a white girlfriend and an immoral life was nothing more than hearsay, I had decided I was going to marry this man.

Later, my father told me everything, just as it had happened. Raju, his father and mine found a fat red couch all the way down the hallway from the ballroom, right by the cloakrooms. It was not the most ideal location, given that gaggles of pudgy women and their tipsy daughters seemed to be spending more time in the ladies' room than at the party.

'So, young man,' my father said to Raju, his disapproving

eye taking in the short spiky hair and defiant gaze. 'Are you enjoying yourself in Bombay? Must be a change from London, no?'

Small talk, but some had to be made before the segue into the next part of the conversation.

'Yes, Uncle, it's nice to come back for family weddings. I've met some nice people.'

'Like my daughter, no?'

'Ha, *ji*, yes. She's a very sweet girl.'

'I know you have gone out alone twice, so I must ask you, what are your intentions for my daughter? Is it not true that you have already discussed marriage? I understand that you asked her today, and that she has been thinking of it. I don't know how things are done in London, young man, but over here a girl's parents must be consulted first. Why did you not consult us?'

Raju's father intervened. 'Please, Gul, these young people today are quite independent in their style. We can't expect them to do what we have done in our day. But if the girl and boy like one another, we should give them our blessings, no?'

'I am not saying that a boy and girl shouldn't be together if they like one another and the families are in agreement,' my father responded tersely. 'But I must be frank. I understand that your son already has a girl. A foreign girl. In London.'

Raju's father suddenly went quiet, a look of exasperation shadowing his face, and shook his head.

'Can you tell me that the reports I have received are mistaken?' my father asked again, this time more fiercely. He could tell by now that Raju was, most definitely, quite drunk.

'It's none of your goddamn business,' Raju spat out, addressing my father. 'I'll bleeding well see who I want to see.' His voice continued to rise. 'And your daughter is a ninny for thinking I was in love with her. I mean, she's all right and all, but the main thing she's got going for her is your money, innit? I just needed to find an Indian wife. The rest of my life is private, out-of-bounds. Got that?' Raju was in such a state of alcohol-fuelled anger, he was hyperventilating.

My father stood up, turned around, and walked back towards the ballroom. He told me later he wanted to cry when he saw me, looking like a peach ripe for the picking, in my pale orange sari. I had taken special care to wear the coral ring that an astrologer had prescribed for me, one that he guaranteed would help clear the path for the right man. For now, however, I was standing alone in my slim column of air and space, pushing down an excitement that kept looping up in my belly, almost unable to hear the banging on the tabla, the wailing notes of the harmonium, the silky strains of the sitar that played near me. Dilbagh Singh was crooning a song of love, written especially for Vikram and Mira. '"There will never be another like you,"' he sang in Hindi. '"There will never be a love like this."' And the couple swooned, buoyed by Johnnie Walker, held aloft by Smirnoff, convinced by the fumes of liquor that there would never be another moment quite like this. I closed my eyes and saw myself and Raju just as Vikram and Mira were now. Happy. In Love. Anticipating a wedding.

My father strode towards us and told us it was time to leave.

In hindsight, I suppose I should have known better.

It wasn't just Uncle Jeevan who seemed to have the inside scoop on Raju's private life. As it turned out, a lot of people did.

Her name was Lucy. They had been together for three years. She played hockey and liked to travel. Raju had promised her that he would drape her in silk saris and garland her with roses when at last he brought her to India to meet his family.

I found out all this when Vikram called the next day, wanting to speak to Anil, and I happened to answer the phone.

'Listen,' Vikram said, awkwardly, still sounding hung-over, 'my cousin Raju feels really bad about all this. He's not a bad guy actually, just a little confused. Don't take it personally, huh?'

I shouldn't have encouraged the conversation further, knowing that whatever Vikram had to tell me would probably only cause me more grief. But I didn't understand what had transpired over the last couple of days, and was looking for some reassurance that it wasn't all my fault.

'Just tell me, Vikram,' I started. 'If Raju has a girlfriend, why did he lead me on?' The tears started to accumulate, but I quashed them. Raju evidently didn't care about me, so I needed to pretend that I didn't care about him either.

'He really loves this Lucy,' Vikram explained. 'But his parents are praying that it will end between them. So we thought he could come here, find a girl, and forget about her. Last week, before he left London for Bombay, they had a huge fight. She expected to come with him. When he said no, she called him a bastard and slammed the phone down. Maybe he thought they were finished, I don't know. He should have been honest with you. I'm sorry. I should have said something at the beginning, but I think we were all hoping he would drop this Lucy and marry you.'

That should have made me feel better but it didn't. Because then, Vikram said something that hurt even more than what had happened the night before.

'Other Bombay girls said no to him because they had heard about the girlfriend. But then we thought of you, that maybe you wouldn't care so much. It's not like you have so many choices, no, Anju?'

Chapter Fifteen

As the Remover of Obstacles, (Ganesh) is frequently propitiated by worshippers suffering from an almost unlimited range of calamities, and also at the start of a ritual or beginning of a journey.

Hindu Gods and Goddesses by A. G. Mitchell

My room door stayed closed for most of the next day.

'*Beti*, come out now. Enough,' my mother implored through the plank of painted wood.

'I'm fine, Ma. Just leave me alone,' I replied.

'Stupid boy!' my mother exclaimed angrily to whomever happened to be in the living room at that time. 'How dare he! What does he mean? He took her out twice, for hours and hours! What does he mean he's not interested in being married! Just wait. Wait until I speak to his mother! I'll give them all a piece of my mind!'

I glanced over at the visualization tape next to my bed. The last time I'd used it was before we had left for the party the night before, when I meditated and imagined Raju and I being congratulated on our engagement.

What crap. I must throw that tape away.

'How dare he waste our time like that, raise our hopes,' my mother continued ranting. 'Take out a good, decent girl, with no intention of marriage. I'm going to jolly well tell his mother a thing or two, stupid woman. Stupid people.'

My mother's vocabulary of insults didn't extend much past 'stupid', so these were fighting words. But truly, there was nothing to be done for it. I had cried enough, and was suddenly tired of being the silly, sad girl who fantasized too much and thought that her salvation resided in a coral ring set in gold.

There was no real reason for me to leave my room thereafter. I certainly wasn't about to go to the wedding, or the last party that was to take place the night before it. My parents didn't push the issue, silently endorsing my decision to stay home. My mother, in a show of solidarity, didn't want to go either, but my father convinced her that Vikram's parents really shouldn't be punished for having an idiot of a nephew. They would go and hold their heads high, even though by now all of Bombay would know that this latest attempt to marry me off had gone spectacularly wrong.

Once they were all safely out of the door, I emerged. I sat in the living room for a while, and dined on the comforting peas-*pulao* and *dahiwada* that Chotu had prepared for me. '*Bimari hai?*' he asked, querying if I was sick. Sick in the head, I wanted to reply. Sick in the heart. Sick of falling in love at the touch of a hand, the merest show of kindness. So sick with envy at Vikram and Mira's gilt-glazed bliss that I found myself hoping it would all come horribly undone. Maybe Mira would find out that Vikram had some woman stashed away – hadn't he been seeing that toothpick-shaped Goan model just last year? Or maybe he would realize, the morning of the wedding, that he didn't love Mira enough. Or that he was a latent homosexual. *Something*, anything, to make *someone* else as miserable, if not more so, than I was at this moment.

I was so sick, in fact, that I decided it was time to go back to New York.

And so started what I called my 'New, New Beginning'. Prior to this, I'd had half a foot in New York and the balance of my limbs in Bombay. As of now I was determined to become a thorough New Yorker.

No looking back. No Bombay madness and matrimonial shenanigans. No neurotic parents. No tacky weddings where there was more booze and jewels than love.

But first, I had to break the news.

My father, predictably, virtually threatened to disown me when I announced my decision. 'I thought that craziness was over!' he boomed. 'You're back here now! What do you mean you're leaving again?'

I started to weep at the table where we had all just finished dinner.

'I can't be here, Dad,' I sobbed. 'I feel so lonely. At least in New York I feel like somebody, not a burden to society like I am here. Please, Dad, try and understand.'

'I thought you gave up that apartment where you were staying,' my mother offered, equally upset. 'So if that's the case, where will you go? I'm sure Lal and Vinita don't want you.'

Anand and Anil – usually my allies – were quiet, afraid to participate in this latest family drama. I knew they didn't agree with what I was doing, but at least they could understand it. I could tell that they both even felt slightly relieved that I was considering going back soon. Having me here these past few weeks had laid a pall over the house, brought a sulk to our mother's face, a worry to our father's eyes.

'No, I didn't give up that place. My friend is house-sitting. She's staying there,' I said, grateful that Sheryl's apartment had been painted that fortnight.

'You didn't tell us that you had any plans to go back,' my mother accused.

'You never asked me, Ma,' I retaliated, tears returning. In the kitchen, Chotu and his entourage were intrigued. They didn't understand exactly what was going on, but knew that it had something to do with marriage. 'I came here, I was willing to stay. I thought I'd find a boy. I thought I did find one. But I didn't, did I? He was a loser, like all the guys that come here,' I said bitterly.

My father sighed deeply and spoke calmly now.

'One bad apple doesn't spoil the bunch,' he pronounced,

having a *Reader's Digest* moment. 'You can't blame all boys just because one was a mistake. OK, so we tried, and it didn't work. We'll try again. But we can only do something if you're here. You promised me the first time we let you go that it would only be for one year. Then you stayed longer. Now you're telling me you want to go back there? For what, *beti*? America is full of Americans and they have strange ways. They are not our type of people, and we are not theirs. Better you stay here, and we'll look after you until God finds you a husband. *Bas*.'

And with that, he stood up, flung his napkin onto the table, and made his way to the sofa, ready to begin that night's television-watching.

I turned to my mother.

'Ma, please,' I begged, pleading with her frigid expression. She looked at me and the disappointment on her face was clear.

'Letting you go away again is not the answer,' she said resolutely. 'It's been bad enough for your reputation so far, and I won't sit here and let people say the things they are saying about you. That you are alone over there, doing God knows what. Already here people were talking about you and Raju because you went out twice alone. They must be thinking that we have done a bad job bringing you up. So we'll take you tomorrow to see another swami, and we'll get you some *seva*, and, *bas*, with blessings, everything will be OK. Don't cry now.'

She too rose from the table and went to join my

father on the sofa, leaving me with my two speechless siblings.

'What?' I asked as they stared at me.

'Nothing,' Anil muttered. 'Look, I know it's hard but—'

'You know nothing about how hard it is,' I snapped back. 'You boys are treated like royalty everywhere. Anand and Anil. Anand and Anil. Everyone always wants to know where you are, what you're doing. You are everyone's favourites; you can get married with the snap of a finger if you want. So don't tell me you know it's hard.'

I got up from the table and went to my room, shutting the door loudly.

The next morning, it was like none of it had ever happened.

By the time I came out of my bedroom, my father was fidgeting with his tie in front of a hallway mirror and waiting for the driver to buzz him from downstairs. My mother was on the phone with Aunt Jyoti discussing the menu for an upcoming dinner party, and both the boys were already at work.

A tape of cymbals and flute music was playing on a stereo in the corner, making me feel sleepy again. Outside the open windows, horns had been honking for hours now, and the cawing of crows perched on the ledge irritated me.

Not that it would have taken much to irritate me today.

250

I wanted to call a friend and meet for coffee and talk about Raju and what had happened. I even thought of calling Raju, but that would be stupid. Plus, he'd probably left by now, to go back to London and his girlfriend. So there really wasn't anyone for me to phone except for Sheryl, and I'd have to book a long-distance call through an operator and then wait – it was such a complicated process.

The *jamandhar* was cleaning the bathroom floors with a hard-bristled brush and lime water, swooshing the liquid contents of her metal pail over the white tiled floors and then scrubbing, scrubbing. She probably had a husband, I thought. She, with three missing teeth and calloused hands and dark, worn skin, crouching on her haunches every day cleaning countless bathrooms in this building. Even she had managed to woo someone.

'*Kuch kao?*' The cook's offer of breakfast was tempting, and I asked him to fix me a big hot bowl of *kichdi*: soft rice with bits of lentil, heaped with yogurt and a sprinkling of crisp fried twigs of batter. This was the real comfort food, the ancient precursor of Häagen-Dazs and a cure for anything from abdominal surgery to a rejected heart.

My mother didn't look up from her phone conversation as I sat alone at the table spooning *kichdi* into my mouth and reading the *Indian Journal*. There had been a break-in at a nearby carpet store yesterday, and the reporter delivered the news with Bollywood-esque drama.

251

CARPETS STOLEN IN DARING
NIGHT-TIME HEIST

Witnesses say they spotted the culprit dashing from the scene of the crime at around nine p.m. He was scared-looking. After some minutes, a truck followed him down the street. The culprit jumped in and the truck raced off. Police inspectors believe the truck was carrying the carpets. The shop owner, Mr Mahir Shah, said about one crore of carpets was stolen. 'This was a most grand caper,' said Mr Shah. 'I believe it was most certainly an insider's job, and am today going to accuse all my staff.' Police have no leads. They have pledged that they won't give up until the culprit has been trapped and firmly punished.

'Pulitzer-Prize-winning stuff,' I mumbled, smiling. In New York, Mr Shah's staff would have slapped him with a dozen lawsuits by now.

I would miss this place. But I had to figure out a way to leave gracefully. This whole episode with Raju had hurt me deeply – more deeply than I cared to share with my parents or anyone else. It had proved to me that despite the sincerity of my intentions and my willingness to please, despite me getting all dressed up and putting myself 'out there', I still couldn't find the man for me. My time in New York had changed, brightened and enlightened me and I needed more of it. What I wanted for my life was important, but so were the good wishes of my parents.

And then it came to me.

I quietly slipped out of the house. Quickly, I found the nearest of the STD booths – little cubicles set up adjacent to food stalls and on random street corners for people who had no telephones in their homes. I waited patiently outside, shielding my eyes from the sun, as someone in front of me yelled loudly into the black receiver, demanding to know from his wife in Ahmedabad when she was coming home. When it was my turn, I wiped the ear and mouthpiece with my handkerchief, and dialled Sheryl's number.

After a twenty-minute conversation, I hung up and paid for the call. Next, I phoned Udhay the astrologer.

Three days later, a FedEx package arrived. Carefully slitting open the envelope, I pulled out a sheaf of papers containing the kind of information that only Sheryl, bless her, could dig up. There were photocopies of magazine articles, lists of statistics culled from various sources, names and numbers and ages that pointed to one critical fact: that I had a better chance of meeting a nice Indian boy in America than I did in India.

That afternoon, on schedule, Udhay called to speak to my mother.

'I've been looking at your daughter's chart,' he said,

thoughtfully. 'Something has come up. Timings have changed. Must tell you. I can come see you now. Vill you send me your driver?'

Two hours later, Udhay was sitting next to my mother on our couch, astrological charts and almanacs spread out on the coffee table in front of them.

'Before you begin,' my mother said quietly, 'it seems all you've been saying these years has been wrong. You told me I would find a boy for my daughter after twenty-six. Now, she's almost twenty-eight. You said if she kept Shiva's fast and did her prayers, a good boy will come. She has done so much, *bechari*, and no boy has come – good, bad, nothing. I know this is not in your hands, Udhay *ji*, but tell me something true, no?'

Udhay bristled.

'Firstly, Leela memsahib, I told you after twenty-six, but I didn't say when after, nah? It could be twenty-eight, twenty-nine only. But see, I found something yesterday, with God's grace, just as I happened to be looking again at your daughter's chart. See this.' And he pointed to a spiral he had drawn, with numbers written in Sanskrit scattered around it.

My mother shook her head.

'It means that she vill only find her God-given intended ven she departs from these shores. He is from owerseas, but she can only meet him owerseas. Not here. He is not coming here. They vill meet in a big city vith plenty cars and foreigners around them. But he vill be a good boy, nice boy, Indian boy. You vill approwe. But first, you must let her go.'

'She has been saying she wants to return to Umrica,' my mother said quietly. 'But her father and I don't believe in it. We don't want to let her go. She will become spoilt over there, all alone, too many freedoms. She was there already, for more than one year. But nothing happened, no boys. Why to let her go again? Better she stay here with us, where we can keep an eye on her, no?'

'She is a different type of girl,' Udhay said, leaning back. 'She vill require a different type of boy. Not for her these mummies' boys. She will find her own boy, and also he vill be independent-type, like her. I can see in her chart, that vith God's grace, she vill meet him soon, if she goes there, mixes, goes to Indian parties, but still do her prayers and fasting. She must especially pray to Ganesh. Yes, Ganesh is very important in her chart just now. Then, *bas*, boy vill come,' he concluded, clapping his hands.

My father and brothers arrived home just as Udhay was leaving. '*Namaste ji.*' The astrologer folded his hands in front of my father, and scurried out of the door.

'Why was he here?' my father asked my mother later, as he peeled off his socks and rubbed his feet.

She filled him in, while he listened quietly but sceptically, uttering 'Nonsense' under his breath.

*   *   *

After dinner that night, I brought out the papers.

'Look,' I said, presenting the facts. 'Did you know there are hundreds of Indian bankers in New York? And engineers? And business people? Not just in New York, but all over the country? Look, they run their own companies. Very successful, educated. Look.'

My parents didn't. Instead, they glanced at one another, and my father began presenting some feeble argument about the 'type' these boys were, probably from the wrong caste or culture. It wasn't enough just to find an Indian boy, he lectured me, but he must be the *right* sort. 'Of our own kind.'

My mother sighed and nudged my father.

'Now, you can't be so fussy any more. Doesn't matter if the boy is not from our type of background. As long as he is good, no? And Hindu. Let's have faith in Lord Ganesh, and let her go.'

PART THREE

Chapter Sixteen

What was the world coming to when acres of newsprint were devoted to Givenchy's dayglo knickers?

Front Row by Lisa Armstrong

'You sly bitch,' Sheryl said, smiling and shaking her head as she shut her eyes and let droplets of sweat dribble from her forehead down her face. We were enjoying a post-workout sauna, and marvelling at the fact that I was back in town.

'What?' I replied, in mock incredulity. 'What did I do? OK, so I paid off an astrologer and asked you to dig up supporting evidence – thank you, by the way. But what else was I supposed to do? I'd still be hanging around my house in Bombay, eating parathas and begging my family to let me leave again.'

'Your poor parents. They probably didn't even see it coming,' Sheryl tut-tutted.

'I felt bad, trust me, really I did. I don't like misleading them. But I did ask the astrologer if anything untoward would happen to me if I came back here, and he checked my charts and said no, it would all be fine.'

'You *paid* him to tell you that!' she laughed. 'What did you think? That he was suddenly going to develop integrity and tell you the truth?'

'He just didn't see anything wrong with it, is what I'm saying,' I replied, firmly. 'Anyway, I'm here now, so no point discussing it, no?'

I had been back in New York for four days, and had never felt happier.

Since pulling what Sheryl would ever afterwards refer to as 'the ultimate Indian-girl scam', I'd convinced Marion to sponsor me for an H-1 visa – a term now a firmly entrenched part of the sub-continental lexicon. It was going to take some time to get it all squared away, and I would be responsible for the bulk of the expenses, but at least I would ultimately be a part of the New York working community, fair and square.

Later, I returned to my studio apartment, which in the evenings filled with red and yellow light flashing from a neon sign depicting a slice of pizza across the street. I was still in that jetlag-induced haze, sleeping lightly and then heavily, waking to senseless dreams about Raju and Vikram, sapphires and sweets. In a corner was a pile of magazines that had accumulated in my absence: *US Weekly* and the *National Enquirer*, and all I could manage to do in the evenings when I got home from work was watch re-runs of daytime television and read self-help books. I called that time my 'Oprah–Chopra Hour'.

But what a joy it was to be back. At seven every

morning, my alarm went off as I heard the cleaners swooshing down the sidewalks, and I drowsily watched Katie Couric introducing the latest high-tech hearing aid. I loved the way the pellets of water felt against my skin as I showered, the fluffiness of towels that hadn't been beaten to death by the local *dhobi*, the way I could go to work in crisp trousers and a T-shirt and my favourite sandals – the ones with the white plastic daisy on the front. It was OK to wear clothes that showed my upper arms, and sometimes maybe even a bra-strap. I stopped every morning at Gabe's, the coffee shop around the corner, and bought a cappuccino and a bagel, which I devoured on the subway while reading the *New York Times*. By nine, I was at my desk, calling editors, selling ideas, organizing photo shoots. And I could write an entire press release and not once use the phrase 'classic with a twist'. This, I thought, was a great leap forward not just for my own career, but for the field of fashion publicity in general.

'You made it back. I have to confess, I had my doubts,' Marion said at a birthday lunch for Erin, a few days after my return. 'Thought for sure they'd marry you off without your consent and that you'd send me a postcard from your new home in Pakistan or wherever. But I gotta say, I'm glad to see you again. The office wasn't the same without you.'

I beamed. 'Really?' Wow. Nobody had ever missed me before, except for maybe my parents, and that didn't count.

We were drinking sparkling wine – Marion claimed to be teetotal but made an exception for staff birthdays and other special occasions, which were often. I felt the bubbles rise to my head and pop. I let out a silent burp before continuing.

'I had a nice time back home. Went to this amazing wedding. My brothers' friend Vikram and a young girl called Mira. They had ten parties in one week. The bride's father wanted to show that he had money. He has a younger daughter, you see, so he was hoping that someone would come forward for her, enticed by the stacks of cash he was throwing around.'

'Did anyone?' Erin asked.

'Don't think so. She's only seventeen and has buck teeth, poor thing. I think her parents are going to send her here for dental work, but they are scared she'll never want to leave. You know, like me.' I giggled. I was having so much fun. I could never talk like this back home.

'You must be such an anomaly, darling,' Milo ventured, sucking on an olive from his salad. 'Poor sweet baby. All alone in the big bad city. No husband, only daddy's money to keep you cosy at night,' he said, bitchily.

Marion, ignoring him, turned her attention back to me.

'Well, we're happy to have you back. And just let me remind you that it's time to let go of the old beliefs and expectations imposed upon you, and discover what you are really here for, what your spiritual purpose in life is,' she said. Her days as a rebirther were not so far behind her, despite the sleek grey Jil Sander suit she now wore. 'You are your own woman, dear. A man will never complete you, and one day you'll see that. You'll find your place in this world, husband or not. If marriage happens, great. But don't make it what your life is all about, OK?'

'How very inspiring,' Milo said, snidely.

I looked around. Marion was twice divorced. Erin, at thirty-two, was single and hadn't had a date in a year. Milo was as bent as an old one-dollar bill, and fantasized about converting stridently heterosexual men. Kris was going through a separation. Last week, Linda discovered that her long-term boyfriend was having an affair, and had had to take a leave of absence because of her nervous breakdown. I should have been discouraged and depressed, but I was not. It may have been the sparkling wine, but I felt stronger and more solid than I'd ever done in my life.

Sheryl had asked me once what defined me, and I didn't have an answer for her. Now I did: not my parents, not my quest for a husband, not my quaint religious endeavours. I was going to be defined by the work I did, the people I befriended and the impact that I would have in my small, but increasingly happy, world.

*   *   *

265

'Paris! Me! Really?' I gasped in delight.

Marion had summoned me into her office and bestowed upon me a magnificent opportunity. Our new client, hotshot fashion designer Len Maverick, had just received serious backing from a multi-national conglomerate and was going to throw the Mother of All Fashion Shows, the Party of the Century, in the City of Lights. Someone from the agency had to go with him, and to accompany the handful of American journalists he was flying over for the occasion.

Three weeks later, I was at the front of the Air France check-in counter at JFK. I was escorting Len Maverick's VIP guests: Anastasia, Jilly, Rose and Penny, all editors at New York's most prestigious magazines. They were all, without exception, blonde, reed thin, and clad in travel-friendly black. They all did the kissy-kissy thing as they congregated at the counter, but gave each other a serious scrutiny when no one was looking.

'Mint?' Jilly offered. She was often referred to as 'Silly Jilly', especially after one notorious appearance on a celebrity television quiz show when she said that Iwo Jima was a hot new Japanese restaurant in SoHo.

The girls secretly hoped they wouldn't have to sit next to one another. It wasn't every day they got to fly first class, and they certainly didn't want the experience sullied by being forced to make conversation the whole way over. No, they all wanted to load up on the free champagne, watch the movie and daydream about one day taking over *Vogue* and being able to fly on Concorde every week.

On board, I went over the pre-show notes and seating assignments. This was a massive responsibility: overseeing all the American media for this designer's first show in Paris; getting the press releases out, organizing photographic shoots, co-ordinating interviews, and entertaining this little posse of girlies for the next couple of days. I looked out of the window as the plane lifted seamlessly off, and felt, for the first time ever, that I may actually now be a grown-up.

'Oh, we had the usual dramas checking into the hotel. One room wasn't ready, another one was smaller than the others, the girls were pissy because they were tired and cranky and felt they weren't given enough of the red-carpet treatment.' I was debriefing Marion about the last twelve hours.

'I know it's frustrating,' Marion soothed. 'But you do need to coddle them a bit. They want to feel special, like the celebrities they write about. Just get inside their heads and try and anticipate what they need, OK?'

'Fine, whatever you say,' I sighed. It was time to shower and prepare for my meeting with Len Maverick.

He was waiting for me downstairs, a lanky, somewhat elastic-looking figure dressed all in white, his head shaved so exquisitely that the crystalline beams from the chandelier above bounced off his scalp.

'So great to meet you, honey,' he said. 'Good flight?'

With silver loops glinting in his sharp Mr Spock-like ears and shiny white teeth that gleamed brilliantly even from across the lobby, he looked a bit predatory. But Milo, who was clearly in love with the designer, had insisted he was 'a sweetie'. He just had to be treated right, Milo had said.

'So, how are the plans for the American press?' he asked, as we settled into a corner settee in the lobby and motioned for a couple of Kir Royales. 'This is a huge deal, honey, you know,' he continued. 'Can't mess up. The journalists need to be happy and write absolutely glowing things, you know what I'm saying? Else, somebody will be held accountable.' He fixed his cool gaze on me.

'I understand, Mr Maverick, sir, but what if they just don't like your designs?' I asked.

He stiffened. Then a smile eased across his thin face. 'Ha, a PR girl with a sense of humour. I like that. Scared me there for a sec, honey. Thought old Marion had sent across some clueless naïf.

'You need to be on top of your game here,' he went on. 'Offer the girls anything they want. If you notice their eyes brightening especially at one of the majestic pieces I'm going to show, it's theirs. Know what I'm saying? This is my debut, the new owners are watching very closely, and I'm not going to blow it. They need to write fabulous things, and it's your responsibility.'

*   *   *

I didn't sleep that night. There was the jet-lag of course. And the fact that my parents, whom I had called right before leaving New York, were more appalled than usual. This time, their daughter was flying alone to another strange country, staying in a hotel by herself, vulnerable to God knows what. What if someone saw me?

'Ma, nobody is going to see me,' I told them before I left New York. 'I don't think any of your friends are going to be at a Paris fashion show. Just relax, OK? I'm only going for a few days and then I'll be back in New York.'

'Is this going to be a regular thing?' My father was on the phone now, sounding gruff. 'Because if it is, you can jolly well tell your boss that you can't do it. I won't allow you to fly here and there by yourself. Understood?'

'It's fine, Dad, it's just this once. Really.'

I replayed that conversation in my head while I tried to battle sleeplessness, which only contributed to my state of high mental agitation. Then there was Len Maverick's demand – quite unreasonable, I thought. Even in my limited experience of fashion publicity, I knew that publicists could hardly control what journalists were going to write, unless it was by way of an all-out bribe – and that certainly wasn't going to happen here. But I also knew a threat when I heard one – and if I didn't come through on this, Marion was almost definitely going to lose the Maverick account, and that would be atrocious. Especially when it was clear that he was on the cusp of monumental international success.

So far, however, everything had gone exquisitely. I'd scheduled Len's one-on-one interviews with the girls perfectly, and they had started and ended on time – a minor miracle. The girls had all been wowed by the sumptuousness of Len's suite at the Bristol. Sitting in an adjacent room so as not to disturb the delicate interview process, I listened to the girls gush over the new line, a few pieces from which the designer deigned to show them early, allowing them to feel as if they'd entered a special circle of privilege. I heard the light tinkle of laughter as Len repeated some vicious fashion-related joke and each girl, one after the other, giggled knowingly, pleased to be part of the conspiracy. I heard the usual give-and-take of buzz words: 'inspiration . . . style . . . antifashion . . . romanticism . . . modernism . . . Paris chic . . . New York commercialism . . . creative spirit . . .' until I couldn't listen any more, and helped myself to the contents of the mini-bar. Each girl was thrilled to be kissed on the cheek by the designer, convinced they were the only ones to have had quite this much attention. They had all received white roses, in full bloom – white was his signature colour after all – in their hotel rooms early this morning, each with a hand-written note. I knew each one had slid the note into their respective Filofaxes to show their friends. Later, they all knew, some wondrous gift would await them in their rooms – perhaps a full-size bottle of his new perfume with complementing bath salts and shower gel, or the tiny dyed-white crocodile clutch bag that was destined to become the must-have of the season. Something luscious, they knew.

Relieved that the first instalment of Project Maverick had gone off well, I was looking forward to receiving the girls at the table I had booked at L'Avenue. They would then have the afternoon free – and would hopefully use the thirty per cent discount they had been given at the Len Maverick store nearby – before needing to be ready for tonight's show, and post-*défilé* soirée. I had already met with Javay, Len's flame-haired Paris-based publicist, and, after a bout of heated squabbling, firmed up my four centre front-row seats.

'Look, Len Maverick is American and it is imperative that our top American journalists are seated in the front row,' I insisted. 'I'm sure you understand that. It would be the same if Yves Saint Laurent came to show in New York.'

''Ee would *never* do zat,' Javay spat out, clearly disgusted at the thought. 'But *bon*, you 'ave your seats. Be zere on time, 'owever, or I will give zem away to Madame Figaro.'

These girls are quite fun once you get to know them, I thought as I helped myself to another glassful of Cabernet. Once they'd all had a couple of champagne cocktails and were awaiting their steak tartares – the house speciality – they were even actually likeable.

'So, you're vegetarian then, are you?' Anastasia asked, after I ordered a platter of steamed carrots, broccoli and spinach. Not the most imaginative fare, but, aside from *pommes frites*, this was the best that a French restaurant could muster.

'Not really. I do eat fish and chicken, but today's Monday and it's a special day for us in religious terms, so no meat allowed. Actually, no alcohol allowed either, but I'll break that little rule today,' I giggled. Strictly speaking, I should have been fasting today but I was feeling slightly reckless, and hungry, and gosh, I was in Paris!

Thus began quite a lively discussion about my religious constraints and how adhering to them would, ultimately, bring me the husband of my parents' dreams.

'Oooh, oooh, I have someone for you!' Penny suddenly announced. 'He's got to be Indian, right? Well, I know this really nice Indian guy. Lives in New York, actually.'

'Oh?' I replied.

'Yeah, he's really sweet. Very polite. And I think he told me one time that his parents were wanting to take him back to India to find a wife for him. So it could be perfect!'

'How do you know him?' I asked, thinking the mystery man was probably Penny's banker boyfriend's colleague, which would be perfect.

'He's the driver for the car service I use when I go to the airport.'

I just looked at her.

'He drives really well,' she added, stirring the raw egg yolk into the mound of red meat on her plate.

Later, we went shopping. At the Manolo Blahnik store, I couldn't quite decide between the turquoise suede mules and the lime-green stilettos.

'Get both,' Penny suggested.

'Actually, I can really only afford one pair,' I replied.

'How ghastly,' Penny replied. 'That is *so Sophie's Choice*.'

Penny, especially, was quiet when I emerged in the lobby that night before the show. While the girls, without exception, were in various forms of black dress – cigarette pants here, halter top there – I had chosen a white beaded sari with a rich silver border. Around my neck was a choker of miniature old-cut diamonds with matching chandelier earrings. I had debated all afternoon whether or not to go ethnic – I was, after all, here on business. All I had been told by Len's image people was to 'wear white, preferably a pantsuit, preferably one of his'. But I had just started working on the account, and hadn't had the time to get fitted for one, so this was going to have to do. In addition, I told myself, I was representing a New York designer and the cosmopolitan nature of the city – and what said international glamour more resoundingly than 'fabulous designer sari'?

'You look nice,' Anastasia said, her pretty face a mix of surprise and envy.

'Thank you,' I replied, confidently. 'And you all look beautiful. Shall we go?'

I led my posse, like a pedestrian funeral procession, into a stretch limo waiting outside. Penny, sitting next to me, looked at the intricate web of diamonds weaving their way across my neck. 'Nice jewellery,' she said. 'Good idea to borrow something like that. Who lent them to you – Cartier or Bulgari?'

'Neither,' I replied, smiling.

Despite my relative sophistication in these matters, entering a large-scale fashion show in Paris was still a culture shock. It was basically the equivalent of kidnapping a geriatric goat-keeper from Bihar and dropping him off at Disneyland.

Despite all my exposure to magnificence in the shape and form of Indian weddings, I had never seen anything quite like this.

In the first place, the people behind Len Maverick had scored the coup of the decade by obtaining permission to hold the show on the grounds around the Eiffel Tower. Its illuminated majesty served as an incomparable backdrop.

The catwalk was covered in darkness, the beams from the lights overhead resting on the thousand seats laid out, row by row, along the stretch of grounds leading up to the monument. Each seat was covered in white damask, a fresh tulip delicately placed on every one. Occupants of the first three rows were also given white goodie bags filled with Maverick essentials: a small bottle of his new perfume Blanc; a tiny white lacquered pen with the initials 'LM' engraved in silver; a pair of white-rimmed sunglasses encased in a snowy pouch, the whole lot wrapped in platinum ribbons.

A white-clad usherette led us to our seats, which, as per Javay's word, were bang centre-front, the best in the house. Jilly, Anastasia, Penny and Rose assumed the grandeur of their positions.

While a hundred photographers were adjusting their tripods and fiddling with their lenses on a podium right behind us, a handful of paparazzi had gathered at the front row on one side of the catwalk, jostling one another for space while desperately clicking away. The object of their attention was Tara Night, a delicious Hollywood actress flown in by private jet for this event. Her hot factor at the moment was positively scalding. She flirted with the cameras – crossing and uncrossing her gazelle-like gams, thrusting out her hefty bosom – all the while pretending not to notice the paparazzi.

I saw, from my standing-in-the-aisle vantage point, that everyone seated in that coveted front row had a bored, slightly menacing look about them. Occasionally, when one of the socialites, semi-celebrities or power-hungry fashion writers saw someone they wanted to speak to, they'd mouth a quick 'Hi, how are you?' without waiting for the answer. It reminded me of the social ladder in Bombay.

Around me, minions bustled. The show producers, all identified by their identical white suits and matching berets, looked as if they were in the throes of some state of national emergency, rushing up and down between aisles, consulting clipboards, speaking into sleek little headsets and walkie-talkies. Music from the new Red Hot Chili Peppers album boomed through invisible loudspeakers, while Maverick and his lackeys backstage made the last-minute preparations. The show had been scheduled to start half an hour ago, but part of the planned drama of these things was always a delay, during which anticipation could build.

Willa Strand was standing in an aisle, looking confused. I recognized her from her pictures in *Vogue* and the *New York Times*. She was a one-time vaingloriously powerful fashion editor who had since been demoted and dumped after it was discovered that she was demanding valuable goodies from fashion houses in exchange for coverage. As a result, she was now a sad, sixty-five-year-old fashion relic. Years ago, all the world's designers had been at her feet. Today, they didn't even speak to her. She certainly couldn't have received an invitation to this event – I had once heard Milo cattily remark that Willa Strand wasn't even worth the cost of the stamp on an envelope. Somehow, though, she had inveigled her way in. I saw one of the ushers leading Willa by the hand – like someone steering their granny through a crowded market – before abandoning her in one of the aisles. I felt sorry for her.

'Excuse me, Ms Strand,' I said, approaching her. 'You look lost. I'm one of the publicists for Len Maverick. May I show you to your seat?'

'I don't have one,' Willa snapped. 'These people, whom I've supported over all these years, treating me this way! Can you believe I never even got my invitation to this show? I'm sure it just got lost in the mail. At least someone outside was nice enough to let me in, but really, they said I had to be in the standing section. What an insult! Who messed up here?'

'I'm very sorry to hear that,' I uttered, 'but let me see what I can do.'

I, frankly, had no power here – my sole jurisdiction was the quartet of girls I was escorting. However, as a Hindu, I'd grown up quite terrified of the ramifications of karma – allow one person to be treated badly, and you can expect the same thing to happen to you, in this lifetime or the next.

But I didn't know where to go for help. The show was about to start – workmen were rolling back the plastic covering on the catwalk, indicating that at last, after an hour's delay, Len Maverick was ready to begin. Scanning the rows and rows of people around me, I spotted a sole empty seat, in the middle of the fifth row, and yanked Willa over.

'There,' I said, hoisting back the *pallav* from my sari, which had begun inching its way down my shoulder. 'Take that seat. It's not as good as you deserve, but it's the best we can do.' I pushed the once grande dame of fashion down the row.

At least a hundred more people were standing at the back, pushed against railings, hoping to see. They were the fashion students, the writers from small-town papers nobody had ever heard of, the friends of Maverick's design assistants. But for all their third-world status, I thought they looked much happier and more enthusiastic than the hard-faced editors in the front row. The people who are delighted with even a standing invitation, who are prepared to wait for hours outside before being let in: those are the real fashion fiends, the ones who deserve the good seats. The front-row inhabitants looked like they were doing the world a favour just by showing up.

I hitched up my sari and found my way back to my group, just as the lights were going down.

To something that sounded like Punjabi *bhangra* fused with Latin high-energy tunes and old-style jazz, a sinuous figure stepped out onto the catwalk, her dark hair wrapped so high it must have added an extra foot to her silhouette. Black and silver glitter rimmed her shining eyes, her ultra-glossy lips reflected the high-intensity light overhead. Her entire frame was draped in a white leather coat, so soft it looked like it had been spun from gossamer, and so long it trailed the catwalk as she strutted its length. I glanced down at my show notes and read that the leather was made from something called 'punched calf'.

'Gosh, poor little thing,' I thought to myself, imagining the animal that Hindus worship being knocked about.

I raised my eyes back to the catwalk, to see a succession of whippet-thin girls, each one more beautiful than the next, slinking down the runway in a series of deliciously sexy clothes. For the next twenty minutes, there was only this: the mesmerizing music, the sharp lights that focused on the runway as if nothing else in the entire universe mattered, and the heavenly clothes that Len Maverick had designed. For those twenty minutes, I was intoxicated, deliriously grateful to be a part of this world, and hoping to become an even bigger part. No wonder fashion people never got out of the business – when there was this much magic, who would ever want to do anything else?

It ended – too soon, I thought – and Maverick appeared on the runway looking tired but triumphant, his skinny arm wrapped around the fourteen-inch waist of one of his models. Everyone in the audience was standing and clapping uproariously. Even with my limited experience of the circuit, I knew that a standing ovation was rare – especially for an American designer doing his first show in Paris. This was going to be all over the papers tomorrow. Thankfully, Len Maverick had practically done my job for me.

When he arrived at the front of the catwalk, he blew a kiss to me and my quartet, all of us swooning with delight at being recognized and acknowledged. It was a transporting thing, this fashion game. If only the people back home could see me now.

An hour later, most of which was spent in our car stuck in disastrous post-fashion-show traffic, I and the girls arrived at Spiro, the hot new club that had been taken over for the after-show celebration.

As soon as we arrived, I wanted to leave. The music was so loud I was certain my eardrums would explode. And if fashion people knew how to do little else, they certainly knew how to handle a cigarette or fifteen; just about everyone in the room was lighting up. The fumes hurt my eyes and, I was sure, were giving me instant emphysema. Dry Martinis were the theme of the evening, each glass brandishing a toothpick speared through a pickled white onion rather than the customary olive – in honour of Maverick, no doubt. The red velvet furnishings had been set aside and replaced with white silk sofas, just for the night, and silvery powder was dusted across the dance floor.

'Enough with the white thing already, right?' I yelled into Penny's ear. She was far too busy chatting up a male model called Gustav to pay any attention.

I detached myself from my charges and found a quiet corner where the cigarette smoking was at a minimum. As I tried one of the Martinis, I remembered life in Bombay, where going to somebody else's engagement party – to inevitably be harangued by all of my relatives – had been the highlight of my week. I had never even dreamt of mixing with people like the ones I was surrounded by here, tonight.

In their midst, I felt proud, independent, one of them. I felt like I was free-falling, but I just *knew* that I would land in the right place.

I drank just enough of my Martini to give myself a soft, gentle buzz – the few sips of vodka would help me sleep tonight. Then I kissed the girls goodnight, left the limo for them, and hopped into a cab back to the hotel.

We were scheduled to fly back to New York the next afternoon.

The girls were all doing their own thing before the flight, so I decided to do something I had never before done in all my life: have a meal in a restaurant alone.

I chose a nearby café and noted that I wasn't the only diner going solo. I ordered croissant and American coffee and some eggs, fished out the paperback I'd brought along, and started to feel like a Really Independent Woman. The book, I had to confess, was to give me something to do so I wouldn't be caught looking awkward or playing with the salt and pepper shakers. But soon I found myself happy to people-watch, comfortable and confident, gazing out of the window.

At the next table, two Americans were talking about

something called pipes and ballasts with all the fervour of Steven Spielberg and Tom Hanks discussing their next big deal. I tried not to listen, but found their conversation fascinating, if only because both these men were living their dreams. They grew up, I imagined, saying to themselves: 'When I get out of college, I want to go into sales for a living.' They probably had sweet wives in Nebraska, wives who would be happy with silk scarf and a little discounted bottle of perfume as a souvenir from their husbands' trips to exotic, glamorous Paris.

Lunch for one was liberating. I felt, well, *anchored* in something that hadn't been there previously.

As I edged the remnants of the scrambled eggs onto my fork with a sliver of toast, the confidence I had started to feel the night before gelled. I could still pray that the man destined for me would come.

But, for the first time, the fact that he hadn't shown up so far was perfectly OK.

Chapter Seventeen

... I looked at the vast numbers of ordinary, non-psychotic women who have faced (and are now just coming to face) that not marrying is not the end of the world.

Women Who May Never Marry by Leanna Wolfe

The phone next to my bed rang early the next Sunday morning. I knew it had to be my mother.

'*Beti,* still sleeping?' she shrilled across the oceans. 'Must be, what, at least nine over there, no?'

'Ma, it's Sunday,' I replied drowsily, heaving myself up off my big fluffy pillow. I was still jet-lagged from my whirlwind trip to Paris last week, but continued to feel a new sense of self.

'So, what are you doing? Going out? Met anyone? Anything happening?' came my mother's regular rapid-fire questions, ignoring my still semi-comatose state.

'Just been busy with work, Ma, nothing else.'

'Hah, OK, actually, I wanted to tell you something I heard. Remember my friend Guni? Who moved to London? Her daughter Seema is a little younger than you? Remember?'

'Yes, Ma,' I lied. 'What about her?'

'So Seema has been in London and she met a very

nice boy from Umrica, and you know how? Through com-pu-ter! Some email-bemail thing. You know what that is, no, *beti*? Everyone is talking about it here. Seema and the boy were writing back and forth on com-pu-ter, and see, then they met at her cousin's wedding in London, and then they got engaged, all in a few weeks, so fast fast. *Beti*, why you're not doing com-pu-ter?'

'Because, Ma, there are mostly just weirdos out there on the Internet. It doesn't work. Maybe Seema was one of the lucky ones.'

'Just try, no? Never know, maybe a nice boy is also on his com-pu-ter looking for a girl. Just try.

'And hah,' she continued, changing the subject. 'Vikram and Mira, remember, that big, big wedding you attended? Mira has gone back to her parents' house, after only a few months. All of Bombay is talking about it. Can you believe it?'

'Why, what happened, Ma?' I asked, feeling a mix of curiosity and vindication.

'Nobody is saying the truth,' my mother suddenly lowered her voice. 'But rumours are that it was, hah, *bedroom* problems.'

I could almost see my mother blushing, thousands of miles away, merely having to intimate that a bedroom factored into a marriage. I smiled, said my goodbyes, sent love to the rest of the family and happily snuggled back under my duvet.

* * *

Three days later at work, my lunch with a new stylist got cancelled, and I found myself in my small office, alone. I'd had a good morning: Len Maverick called again to say how thrilled he'd been with the coverage since the Paris event, and that he had just taken a call from a producer of the *Today* show. Another client, Be-Bop-Bags, had sent flowers thanking me for getting their new collection featured in *Women's Wear Daily*. A hot new beauty brand had written asking if Marion and I would meet with them next week to pitch for the account.

All this, and it wasn't even one p.m.

Satisfied at all that I had accomplished that morning, I logged on to the Internet, and went straight to Desimatch.com, which was considered the 'premier matchmaking site for lost and lonely Indians in far-flung lands'.

'*Hai Ram,*' I said to myself. 'Even in cyberspace, everything is a drama.'

I registered a secret email address, entered the portals of the site, and found garish *mehendi* designs and icons of little women draped in red-and-gold saris and tiny men with turbans wrapped around their heads. This was hard-sell, no doubt about it. It wasn't just about logging on and finding a friend, a date, a companion maybe. It was about finding someone to marry, in just a few easy steps.

Choosing from the various categories and options, I

typed in my requirements: *Age: 30–35; Height: 5'8"–5'11";* *Build: Slim–Average; Complexion: Light-Wheatish. Place* *of Residence: New York–New Jersey. Caste: Sindhi. Reli-* *gion: Hindu. Education: Minimum College Degree.*

There, I thought, sitting back and looking at my entries. Specific, but flexible. Targeted, but not too demand- ing. Just the kinds of criteria my parents would ask for.

I pressed Enter, and waited.

No matches found, came the reply.

'I knew it,' I said to myself. 'I'm not even asking for any special type of a personality, and he still doesn't exist.'

We suggest you widen your search, came the next instruction.

So I did, extending the age factor, lowering the height barrier, even substituting my 'Complexion' submission for 'Dark': hey, the fellow could always use Promise of Fairness. Under 'Place of Residence', I input 'US', figuring I or he could always travel for love. But I wasn't going to budge on the caste and religion thing – I hadn't changed that much.

Eleven matches have been found, my screen said opti- mistically, and I was surprised to feel a little thrill. This could be fun.

I scrolled down.

Hey there, Indian babes [crooned someone who

went by the byline of 'delhistud']. If you can be my salt, I can be your pepper. Together, let's add some flavor to life!

I scrolled some more.

The next potential had included a picture of himself. He was clad all in black, a thick gold chain around his neck, and was reclining on a park bench surrounded by flowers and shrubs. It was a shockingly incongruous image, like Tony Soprano prancing through a meadow.

Hi, ladies, do you think you're the one for me? I'm a manly man, but I like romantic walks on the beach at sunsets! I love flowers and I really want to pluck one of these lovely roses and give one to you! But I can't, if you're so far away! So, ladies, drop me a note and tell me what is in your deepest heart, and let me sweep you away and answer all your prayers!

Thank goodness I had skipped lunch.
I continued scrolling.

I am blameless innocent divorced man. I before have married to crazy-demented white woman, only for purpose of green card. Am seeking wife number two.

I am honest, good person. Please be good and email me by return.'

I laughed. This was *better* than lunch.

In subsequent free time, I continued down the cyberspace path. I had been a de facto New Yorker, on-and-off, for a well over a year now, but had barely even been out to dinner with a man. And I lived in a city – or so I'd argued – crammed to the tips of its skyscrapers with savvy bankers, sophisticated lawyers, clever computer boys, all emigrants from India, all people like myself hoping to find a slice of their homeland in the heart of a compatriot. My uncle and aunt had more or less faded from the picture; they, too, seemed to have given up. And as far as the opportunities for meeting people that my work afforded, they were primarily gorgeous but gay men and the occasional Italian with a bald head, designer stubble, and close-fitting suit. Nice, but not quite what you'd take home to Mummy.

'Sheryl, have you done this Internet matchmaking thing?' I asked my friend one evening over vodka and blinis at the Russian Tea Room.

'I'd like to meet someone, but I'm not that desperate,' Sheryl replied, spooning more caviar onto her tiny pancake. God bless the expense account.

'Oh,' I replied, biting my lip and suddenly feeling, well, desperate.

'Trust me, only losers go on-line.'

'I don't know how true that is – I'm on-line, and I'm not a loser. There are quite a few Indian matrimonial websites now, given the numbers of young Indians in other parts of the world who can't seem to meet anyone. It's a good thing. Speeds up the process.'

Sheryl leant back in the banquette, and sighed.

'Honey, there's only one way to meet someone and that is to get out there. Go to parties, go to bars, go to little dinner parties. Ask friends to fix you up. Flex those dating muscles. All you ever do is write press releases and call Mummy in Bombay. How far is that going to get you? So maybe you won't meet an Indian prince the first time, but how else do you know what's out there unless you give it a go? Have a fling, go away for a weekend, explore, experience. That's what relationships are all about – not about finding a husband on date one.'

I knew what Sheryl was trying to tell me, and I had even started to believe her. There was a lot to be said for the old-country way of doing things – after all, my mother had done it that way and was *perfectly* happy.

But I wasn't my mother, so it was evidently time to try something new.

After a few weeks of checking out three different Indian matrimonial websites, I finally located someone worthy of a response. A thirty-two-year-old businessman in

Houston. I was quite taken by his earnest, straight-forward pitch.

I never thought I'd be doing this, but I know it's time to try something new, as the old methods just aren't working for me. I came to Texas with my family when I was very young, and have lived here ever since. I work in the office supplies business, as a sales manager. I live with my parents, but that will change once I marry. I am an easygoing, fun-loving guy who is a healthy blend of East and West, and I'm looking for a woman with similar values – someone who can happily associate with Americans yet still feel at home in a sari. If you think that might be you, drop me a note. I don't care about height/weight/complexion. I just want to know the kind of person you are.

I did what I always did in such situations, and, before making any moves, called home.

'But what do you know about his family, *beti*?' my mother asked.

'Nothing, but I won't know anything until I get in touch with him. No harm. I won't give him my phone number or anything.'

My father came on the phone.

'What does the boy do?' he asked, sternly.

'He said in his email that he is a sales manager for an

office supplies company. Sounds OK, no?'

'Hmm, door-to-door salesman, is it? How much do you think he'll be making every month? Enough to support you?'

'Dad! I haven't even contacted him yet! Just wanted to let you know what I was doing before I did it. Ay, I'll *never* find anyone if you are going to be so picky. You tell me that I'm choosy, but see what you're doing!'

'*Beti*,' my father soothed. 'At least we are choosy about the important things. You complain if the boy isn't wearing the right socks. But hah, never mind, you send him email-bemail, and find out more. Otherwise, *beti*, everything else is OK?'

After we hung up, I compiled a succession of email responses, each one, I thought, worse than the one before it. If this went on any longer, Mr Tex-Mex would find a wife and have two children before I managed to contact him.

Finally, I settled on this:

Hi. I saw your email listing and thought you sounded interesting. I live in New York, and work in the media. I'm very Indian at heart, but many of my friends are from different cultures and communities. I'm 28 years old, and seeing as you don't appear to care about my vital statistics, I won't share them with you here. But if you'd like to communicate further, I'd be happy to hear from you.

An hour later, a reply.

> Hi. My name is Kumar. What's yours? Shall we
> speak on the phone? Can you send me a photo of
> yourself?

I felt put out. This was the cyberspace equivalent of getting to third-base after a coffee date.

> Hi, [I typed in.] Before we speak or I send you a
> picture, I'd like to get to know you this way. I'd feel
> more comfortable. Hope that's OK.

Before I knew it, we were 'chatting'. Good thing Marion had gone for the day, and things were quiet in the office that afternoon. Kumar seemed personable enough, and at least he could spell. Numerous other listees on the site had even misspelt the word 'marriage', which I thought was a pretty bad sign.

But Kumar was well educated and a good conversationalist; he had a degree from the University of Texas, a managerial position in a national company, a life that seemed to include plenty of friends, weekend barbecues, visits to comedy and jazz clubs. Decent. Nice. A life I could relate to. And, clearly, Kumar was struggling with the same issues: American or Indian, wife or plaything, burgers or *beendi*.

Finally, after an hour of cyberspace-chatting, we decided

to transfer our conversation to a phone line. We would speak the next day, and, if all went well, would agree to meet in a couple of weekends.

'Maybe this is it,' I said excitedly to Sheryl on the phone that evening. 'He just seemed so *nice*. After all this, he could be the one.'

'You haven't even spoken to him yet,' Sheryl responded, sounding exasperated. 'He could be a serial rapist. Hell, I'm sure even Jeffrey Dahmer sounded *nice* to people the first time around. Stop with the delusions already.'

I immediately went on the defensive. I knew I was naïve sometimes, but felt it was one of my more appealing traits. However, not wanting to pursue it until I had met Kumar and proved he was indeed the one, I said, 'Never mind. What are you up to these days?'

'Oh, went out for sushi last night with a guy from my ju-jitsu class. I'd been eyeing him for weeks, very cute. Drives an old Morgan, fabulous. He kept swiping my wasabi. It just really irritated me. And he ate way more salmon roe than me, plus downed his sake in record time, and still expected me to pay half the check. He called this morning, but I don't want to see him again,' Sheryl finished. I could hear her filing her nails on the other end.

'But he was nice, no?' I asked. 'Why don't you give him at least one more chance? I'm not surprised every-one in New York is single and miserable. The smallest thing, and they dump the person. My mother says it's like moving house because you find a cockroach. Total overreaction, no?'

I had much to do in preparation for the phone call to Kumar. I chanted one of my many mantras and did a small Ganesh *puja*. I spent ten minutes performing a spiritual cleansing that would, purportedly, rid my aura of negativity. I lit a pair of pink candles (a symbol of romance and unity) and rubbed my rose quartz (a stone that is said to smooth the path to love). I slipped a Luther Vandross CD into my player and turned down the lights.

This was pseudo-seduction, in lieu of the real thing. I willed myself to be charming, clever, warm, just a little flirtatious. I willed myself to win him over with my words.

At the appointed time, I called, and he picked up instantly. He said it was nice to 'meet' me, and we laughed. He told me about his work, his family, his friends, all the core pieces that make up someone's life. He asked me all about mine. He seemed intrigued by the work I did, the people I met on a daily basis. He thought it sounded glamorous, and not like the 'paper-pushing, literally' that he did. There was a sympathy there, and we both sensed it.

Just as we were discussing when we should talk again, and then consider meeting, he asked me if I had told my parents about this little email-generated alliance. Yes, I said, I had called them.

'Oh, you don't live with them?' he asked. 'I assumed that you did.'

'No, they are in Bombay. I'm here.'

'So who are you staying with?'

'Nobody. I live alone.'

Silence.

'Um, OK,' he stuttered. 'I have to go now. You have my number and I have yours. Let's try and speak again soon, hah? OK, bye.'

I heard a click.

I tried to tell myself that he probably *did* have to hang up, that maybe he had an important call coming in. Of course, I knew better. He'd assumed I was a typical Indian girl, still home with her parents until the day she found a groom. After all, he was still living with his. I knew for sure this was the case when, despite two casually phrased emails telling him how much I enjoyed our chat and how great it would be to do it again, I heard nothing back. Sheryl was wrong: even if Kumar had resorted to the Internet to seek a wife, he wasn't a loser. He was just like every other guy I'd known – scared and closed-minded.

Much later, one of my more sympathetic relatives would repeat the words of encouragement offered to single Indian women everywhere: 'The boy destined for you has been born. You just have to find him.'

After all these years of looking in the real world, it was clear he wasn't to be found in cyberspace either.

Chapter Eighteen

And now we come to the Big Road . . . the Great Road
which is the backbone of all Hind . . . such a River of
Life as nowhere else exists in the world.

Kim by Rudyard Kipling

Thereafter, I fell into a velvet-cushioned rut. Marion was retreating from the PR scene, and was virtually handing over the company to me. We doubled in size and evolved into the most prominent event and publicity enterprise in the city. That one trip to Paris became one of many, enhanced by sojourns in Cannes and Capri, Milan and Munich. Wherever there was a party to be had, a perfume to be launched, a designer to be showcased, we were there.

I had just returned to New York after another drawn-out trip to Bombay, where I had seen my young cousin Nina marry. There, I had considered the notion of life in Accra. I had fallen for a man from Madrid in a photograph. I had promised my parents I would stay, just a little while longer, until – as my father had said – we would 'get the job done'. Two weeks later, I gave up and came back to New York.

My parents, at this point, had no choice but to loosen their grip. My mother continued to fast and pray and chant her mantras, to hope against hope that it would all work out in the end. The constant travelling on my part made such spiritual endeavours almost impossible: it's slightly onerous to perform a *puja* in front of a full moon during a layover in Frankfurt.

I had followed Sheryl's advice, and I was well and truly 'out there', but it hadn't made a difference. I had come to accept that there was a divine timetable about all this. As one psychic in Dubai told me: 'When the time is right, you could be under a rock and he would still find you.'

My brother Anil inched ever closer to the state of matrimony. Any day now, I anticipated, my mother would call to tell me of his engagement, and then she would cry, 'Lord, before I leave this earth, let me also see my daughter married!'

Anil, however, had expectations of his own. He was a resoundingly conservative young man, and knew without being told that a daughter-in-law can make or break a household. He – like Anand – had no intention of ever moving out. The two of them would bring their wives to bear their children in the same house where *they'd* been born, and would be there to care for our parents as they aged.

So Anil was looking for a particular kind of girl, one who would acquiesce to the rules of the household and get along sensationally with everyone in it, yet who had

302

humour and charm and personality. Proposals flooded in for him, and he would consider of each one: 'Will she be as good to my parents as she is to me?'

In the West, he'd be seen as a wimp.

For us, he was a dutiful and loving son, well deserving of all the blessings showered upon him.

He had his quirks though. He disliked girls who were even a little flamboyant, turning down one who showed up at an arranged meeting in a cropped top and sunglasses perched on the top of her head. A few times, if the girl in question happened to be living in the US, I was called upon to veto her. I disliked one because she wore a revealing and somewhat tacky turquoise lace top, and because of a conversational gridlock: all her answers to my carefully thought out questions went little further than 'yes' or 'no' or 'hah, maybe'. Then there was the one that my whole family seemed very keen on, but my brother less so because he couldn't even remember having met her. My parents goaded him to 'just go, just meet her again', which he did, en route praying to Sai Baba for 'a sign'.

She sauntered in, a pair of Ray-Bans holding up her hair (obviously a big fashion statement in Bombay circa 1999) and that was it: he ran screaming for the Malabar Hills.

Not that I ever gave up on myself. Well-meaning relatives suggested I 'lower my expectations'.

'Darling, you're no Cindy Crawford,' said one uncle.

'Eventually, you'll have to take what you can get.'

So while I occasionally gave in to sad daydreams of ending up in a spinster's colony in Pune, wearing polyester dresses and thick tights to cover my hairy legs, I took hope from other people's tales of love found in the unlikeliest of places. I let myself be led from my table at a soirée in Paris by the CEO of a fashion company who said he wanted to introduce me to 'a real Indian prince, and he's single'. The royal in question, short, bespectacled and with fish-lips, turned his head away from me as I smiled a hopeful, happy smile.

I by now had an international group of friends, all of them united in an effort to help me achieve matrimonial status. Their intentions were heartbreakingly sweet. My friend Ava's husband worked in a law firm and had a colleague who, Ava said, was 'Indian, successful, cultured. Perfect for you!'

'We're going to invite him to dinner, but we won't tell him it's a fix-up,' she said. 'That way, it will feel less contrived.'

'Sure, I'd love to come to dinner,' he had said. 'Can I bring a date?'

These things took a highly circuitous route. My friend in Monte Carlo had a former colleague in Boston whose husband occasionally played tennis with someone in New York.

'He's Indian!' my friend rejoiced. 'Apparently very handsome, successful. Perfect for you!'

As perfect as a potential mate might be, however, if he doesn't feel 'that way' about you, there isn't much in your power to be done about it. There were a few such men – the tall-fair-handsome-rich kind that would have made my parents faint in delight. Right pedigree, right background, right everything. Slick, stylish, clean-cut and corporate. BMW and designer-appointed high-rise condo. Right in every sense; it's just that I wasn't right for them.

In the end, I was just me. Striving, enthusiastic, dramatic me. There was the brilliant Indian Stanford MBA who was going to be at a dinner party in New York. Erin told me I just *had* to be there.

'I'm in London that weekend,' I said, consulting my Palm Pilot.

'Fly back,' she insisted.

So I did – but the only way I was going to get back in time was on Concorde. I availed myself of an upgrade coupon, and arrived in New York several hours before the party, giving myself enough time to bathe, pluck, preen, primp and pray. (Same mantra, different schedule.) I also read *The Rules*, the book that everyone was talking about, and resolved to follow all the instructions in it.

At the party, we were briefly introduced and then he went off into the garden and mingled. I sat at the kitchen table and stirred a pitcher of margaritas.

'What are you doing here?' Erin demanded. 'Get out there! Socialize, flirt, at least go *talk* to him!'

'I can't,' I replied quietly. 'In *The Rules*, it said that women aren't supposed to go chasing after men. If he liked the look of me, he'll come in here and find me.'

An hour later, the Stanford graduate took his MBA and left the party, and I was still playing with the glass jug in the kitchen. I strolled outside and sat on a ledge in the garden. I began talking to a nice Jewish guy sitting next to me.

'So, what's your story?' he asked.

'Me? Oh, nothing. I've been out of town. Just got back in today.'

'Oh, so *you're* the Concorde girl!' he said. 'You're the one who flew back to meet the guy who just left.'

'You know about that?' I asked, shocked.

'Know about it? Honey, there's a website devoted to all your efforts,' he joked. 'People are placing bets. They're making predictions. They're writing reviews. They're offering advice.' He laughed – but in many ways it was true. I had become known as the girl in search of a husband and wasn't ashamed to show it.

They say that you find the love you seek when you stop looking. They say that the second you get busy with work, friends, other interests outside romance, the man or woman of your dreams comes sauntering into your life.

I say they're wrong.

The fact is, when you're looking for love, you can't ever

really stop. The possibility of it lingers in every dinner invitation, at every cocktail party, in every plane-, train- and bus-ride. It hovers in the air each time you attend a wedding, take a language class, occupy a window table at your favourite restaurant. The scent of it beckons from around the very next corner. It could happen tomorrow. It could happen today.

They say these things are destined. They say it is written in the stars, that love appears in many forms, and it's in the discovery of its uniqueness that true bliss is found.

I say they're right.

It happened for me because of a tiny, tight chain of events that started with Madonna. The superstar was lending her name to a glitzy fund-raiser in Los Angeles, and I was one of the organizers. I wore a lilac silk sari and was looking up at podiums on which sculpted women in black bikini-tops and thongs gyrated to music. I was thinking to myself: 'Does your mother know you're doing this?'

Behind me, I heard someone say: 'That's how all women should dress.' He was talking not about them, but about me. His name was Jason and he was an actor. We talked the rest of the evening, and became very good friends.

One afternoon, Jason called me.

'I've met your soul mate,' he said. 'I've met the man you're going to marry.'

I rolled my eyes. 'Thank you, Jason,' I said. 'But others

have tried and failed, so I'm not going to put too much stock into what you're telling me.'

'No, no, no,' Jason insisted. 'Really. He's great. He's Indian too. A nice, open-minded kind of guy. Trust me.'

It turned out that Jason and Rohan had met at a charity volleyball tournament on Venice Beach a few days earlier. They had gone for a beer and burgers afterwards, and Jason had talked about his fiancée.

'I wish I had someone too,' Rohan had said. 'It's no fun being alone at thirty-nine.'

'Why don't you go back to India and find a wife?' Jason had suggested, recalling our many conversations. 'I have a friend, Anju, whose parents—' He stopped, mid-sentence. 'Oh my God, Anju, she's *perfect* for you!'

Jason told me all this over the phone, as I was choosing slides to send to a magazine.

'What do you want me to do, darling?' I asked him. 'I'm in New York. He's in LA. It's probably just going to be another waste of time anyway.'

'Distance never stopped you before,' Jason reminded me. 'After all, you were about to marry a man in West Africa, for God's sake.'

Two days later, an email arrived. *Jason has spoken glowingly of you*, said the words on my screen. *Maybe we can connect?*

The emails flew back and forth, superficial at first (place of birth, profession, interests) and then growing deeper, warmer, more probing. He was California-born, had been there all his life. His parents lived an hour away from his home in LA, and I laughed when he told me they called him *sixty million times a day*. He cared not one whit that I lived alone in New York, my own parents an ocean away.

That's great, he had written. *What an accomplishment. You should be proud of yourself.*

We decided to speak on the phone the following day. For once, I performed no special rituals, lit no candles, said no prayers. Whatever was going to happen with this, was going to happen with this.

We talked every day for two weeks (my phone bill had to be delivered to me on the back of a lorry) and decided it was time to meet. But first, he had a request.

'I'm not saying anything to my parents about this,' he said. 'I ask you to do the same.'

'Why?' I had asked. I knew the answer: that telling either one of our families would be like broadcasting something on CNN. In a matter of minutes, calls would be made across my motherland and seep out into the rest of the world, specifics would be asked for, reports faxed around, details given, astrologers consulted. My parents would want to know *everything* about him, his about me. It would become a 'relationship-by-auntie-committee' – and Rohan was having none of it.

'We need to be two independent people in this,' he had said. 'That's the only way we can see if it is going to work.'

It killed me, but I had to abide by his directive. All I wanted to do was give my mother hope, during one of her Sunday morning phone calls, that yes, Ma, there *was* someone! I just wanted to give her some peace of mind that I was doing my bit. Keeping quiet about my life was uncommon – and uncommonly hard.

As serendipity would have it, Marion needed to send me to Los Angeles to research the possibility of opening a second office there. (She had been somewhat spurred on by the fact that there was, at last, a man in the picture.) I told Rohan this, and he whooped with delight.

'Fantastic! I'll meet you at the airport!' he had said.

'Er, no. I was thinking that I could go straight to the hotel and we could see each other there?'

I had it all planned assiduously: I would arrive, relax at the hotel, shower and change and be as fresh as a new rose before I let him lay his eyes on me. When I told him this, he laughed. He said he couldn't wait to meet me, and that he wanted to be the first one to see me as I stepped off the plane. It took vast amounts of courage and confidence on my part to do what would have previously been unthinkable: embark on a 'blind date' with someone immediately after I had undergone a six-hour flight.

So the first time we met was at LAX. I arrived wearing red. He came up to me and hugged me, telling me he had thought it might be me, but wasn't certain because – as he knew about my fashion-heavy lifestyle – he thought that I'd 'have more luggage'.

He stepped back and I took him in, this tall and dark-haired man, his arms heavy with flowers, a tentative smile on his face.

Immediately, it felt right. We *looked* right together. He was the kind of man I would have noticed at a family wedding, and might have asked Maharaj Girdhar about. He was the kind of man that my mother would have called Aunt Jyoti about, the kind for whom orders would be placed for gold coins and Indian sweets covered in silver paper and slivers of pistachio.

And I had found him all on my own. Well, I guess Jason helped.

Rohan was a civil rights lawyer who wrote poetry and played the piano. He was creative, kind, profoundly humane. With him, I didn't care what I wore or if my shoes matched my bag.

Over my five days there, we dined, saw movies, talked quietly for hours at a time. We found a bridge over a brook, sat on it with our legs dangling down, and munched on sweet red watermelon. That was, singularly, the happiest day of my life, the simplest, the most radiant and real.

When I returned to New York, Marion asked me about the feasibility of a West Coast office.

'Oh, that,' I said, absent-mindedly. 'Yes, er, good, I guess. Lots of potential business.'

'You like him that much, do you?' she asked, her rebirthing persona kicking in.

'Yes, Marion,' I replied quietly. 'That much.'

Rohan and I talked that night, and I told him that a stack of new clients and projects was going to keep me in New York for a while.

'But look,' I reassured him. 'I'll come and visit every month or so. We can make it work.'

'Getting on a plane every few weeks – that's not the kind of relationship I want to be in. It's *not* going to work.'

He told me that being in the same city was a non-negotiable. So I did what every other successful and single New York female would do: I suggested he move to *my* city.

'Come and live here,' I encouraged him. 'Loads of jobs, you'll find something quick.'

He said no. His father was unwell and he, being the only son, needed to be close at hand.

Marion knew what was happening, without being told.

'Look, Anju,' she cooed. 'I think the Los Angeles office is a really workable idea, and I think you'd be the best person to run it.'

I sighed, and considered my options. Either I could stay here and regularly monitor the website that had been set up to chart my matrimonial escapades, or I could spend some time in Los Angeles with the man who was, without a doubt, the closest I had ever come to finding 'the one'. Truly, I knew, if he wasn't it, I may as well give up and become a missionary.

Even so, I was annoyed that I was committing to a relationship instead of what I *should* be doing – committing to a marriage. I thought there was no nobility in this – this 'trying things out'. We had spent five glorious days together already – what more did he want?

But Rohan convinced me that if I wanted to see this through, I needed to consider the opportunity that Marion had offered to me.

So a month after Rohan and I had met, I arrived in Los Angeles to take up my new position as 'Vice-President – West Coast Operations' of Marion's company, a very grandiose title given that I worked alone in a tiny sublet off Sepulveda Boulevard.

That night, after he had come over to help me unpack, we went out for sushi.

'You'll be happy here,' he had said to me. 'You know I'll do anything I can to make it easy for you.'

'Well, it's just a matter of time, right?' I asked, stirring some wasabi into a shallow dish of soy sauce. 'I mean, soon we'll have to tell our parents *something* and then we may as well make it official.'

Rohan set down his chopsticks, and looked at me.

'Anju, my dear, I think you're wonderful,' he said.

My heart stopped. Was a break-up looming? He had *just* lured me over, the cad!

'You're wonderful and kind and sweet,' he continued, 'and I'm thrilled and honoured to have a woman like you in my life. But you're mistaken if you think I'm going to do this the way they do it in the old country. I'm not. This relationship is going to unfold in its own time. I'm not going to be dictated to by my parents, or by yours.'

The hot green mustard had seared its way through my sinuses and had brought tears to my eyes. I blinked them back as I scraped sticky grains of rice off my fingers. What was he saying? That I'd be in one of those Western-style things, indefinite and amorphous? I didn't want a *boyfriend*, I wanted to scream at him. I wanted a *husband*!

'My parents are worried about me,' I said quietly. 'First New York, now LA. They don't know what I'm up to. I can't do this to them.' I started to cry.

Rohan reached across the table, knocking aside the small porcelain dishes, and put his hand on top of mine.

'Anju, tell me something,' he said, gently. 'If your parents genuinely didn't care when or if or who you married, would you be here with me? If I didn't meet all your criteria, would we be having this conversation? Tell me, where do your mother's wishes end and where do you begin?'

Now, I couldn't stop crying, and I fumbled through my bag for a spare Kleenex.

'Take me home,' I said quietly, hiding the hysteria that was mounting inside me. I clutched the diamond-studded talisman of the Goddess Durga that hung around my neck and rubbed the coral ring on my finger, as if

314

doing so would melt all the hurt away. 'Take me home right now.'

Two new clients called the next day, but I let my answering machine deal with it. Rohan called three times, but I didn't pick up for him, either.

I was devastated. And I was scared. Rohan could offer me plenty, but he wasn't able to give me what I might have been able to get from an arranged alliance: a guarantee, a ring on a deadline. And he was shutting out my parents in the process – even while knowing that my marriage would herald the end of their sadness. I had told him that the night before, hoping to arouse his sympathy. I had told him how much I loved my parents, and how I *needed* to be married – soon. I had seen the fear on his face when I said that. He said he understood it – after all, he had a younger sister – but that didn't make it right. And it certainly wouldn't convince him.

I wanted to call my mother and tell her all this, hoping that she and my father could fix it, that they would have a relative put some pressure on Rohan's parents, who in turn would lean on him. After all, that was how these things worked.

But of course I couldn't do that – not only because my parents knew nothing of him, but because Rohan deserved better than that.

I neither picked up the phone nor left the house for

three days. This was not something any of my girlfriends or Marion could help me with. This was something I had to figure out on my own.

For hours over those three days, I meditated, chanted, cried and wrote. I sat cross-legged in front of a small granite statue of Lord Shiva, and I repeated the mantra over and over, louder and louder: '*Om Namah Shivaya, Om Namah Shivaya.*' I wanted those words to transport me to a place of peace.

But the mantra was going to take me there the long way. I beseeched the heavens – this time for solace instead of a spouse. As I immersed myself in the resonance of the chant, I felt light-headed, the tears coming in waves, sobs so powerful that they were my only source of breath.

And then I saw it, my massive issue, bright as day. I saw what had been pushing me and pushing me all these years, from where the desperation had come.

My having a 'perfect' mate would, finally, end the regretful sorrow and lasting disappointment in which I believed my parents held me. I was *finally* going to do something to make them love me. And I had to do it fast: my most imposing fear, the fear of the little girl that still lived in me, was that one of my parents would die, leaving the other one alone to shoulder the burden of my singleness. Just thinking of it mired me in guilt.

Rohan had seen all that in me, and loved me anyway.

I finally called him back.

'Hey, I was worried about you,' he said. I caught him right before he was leaving for work. 'I was thinking of coming over to make sure you were all right, but figured you needed to be left alone.'

'I did,' I replied. 'I've needed some time to think. I'm sorry if I pressured you. It was never my intention. It's just . . . well . . . you know how it is.'

'I know,' he said. '*I* have Indian parents, remember? They're freaking out as well. I'm pushing forty. But if we're going to do this, we have to do it our way, and in our own time. And we need to see each other clearly, and not be confused by what our parents want for us. Understand?'

I did, finally.

I also decided to make a trip back to Bombay.

'Aren't there plenty earthquakes in LA?' my father asked, as we drove home from the airport. He had some vague knowledge of my new job running a branch office in Los Angeles, but was still baffled by it. Having not spent much time in the US, he endearingly thought that I could go to work every day in LA, and make it home for dinner in New York.

'It's not too bad,' I assured him. 'So far, so good.'

My mother was waiting for us at home, her hair piled with curlers.

'*Beti!*' she squealed when she saw me. 'You've come

back! *Ay*, so thin you're looking! Eat! Eat!' she said, shoving a chunk of cashew *mithai* into my mouth.

I hugged her, and we all sat down, as Chotu brought out a tea-tray.

For once, she actually asked me how I was. She wondered if my job was going OK. She asked if I liked my apartment in LA, and if I had good friends there. I wondered if she had consumed some elixir that had caused her to forget the fact that I was single, but I was most appreciative of it none the less.

It wasn't to last for long, though. Later, when Anil and Anand returned home from the shops and we all sat around the table for dinner, the matter inevitably arose. This time, however, I had something new – and truthful – to tell them.

'Actually, Ma, Dad, there *is* someone,' I said, ignoring the mound of rice and dahl on my plate.

Everyone fell silent, and looked at me. They could tell, by the expression on my face, that I was absolutely sincere and serious.

'I've met someone, and we really, really like each other. I think it's going to work.'

My mother dropped her napkin and let out a squeal. 'Indian, he's Indian, no, *beti*? Please say he is!'

'Yes, Ma. Indian. Like us. Everything is like us. You'll be happy,' I said.

Then I paused.

'But that's not why I like him. If he was a different

colour, I'd still like him. He's very kind, and clever, and he cares for me.'

My mother pressed her hands together, closed her eyes, and mumbled a prayer beneath her breath. My father reached out for a warm chapatti and my brothers remained quiet and gazed at me.

'I see,' said my father. 'Good for you.'

'I'll let you know what we decide, when the time is right,' I said. 'Please don't ask me about it, and please don't pressure me. If it's meant to work out between us, it will. His name is Rohan, and that's all I'll tell you.'

There were a few seconds of silence, and my parents turned to look at one another. Finally, my father spoke.

'OK, *beti*. We trust you.'

My mother, however, couldn't resist.

'Rohan what?' she asked. 'And is he tall?'

Rohan called very late that night, and we talked for hours. I told him about our family's dinner-time conversation, how *resolved* I felt, how clear. I told him that I saw and respected the purity of our union, mine and his. And then I told him something that convinced him I was ready to be with him. I told him that even if my parents were to object to him for whatever reason, I'd marry him anyway.

'So let's do it,' he said quietly, his voice fading in

and out across the ocean. He paused for a second, as if reconsidering his words.

'My dearest Anju,' he began, 'would you do me the stunning and colossal honour of becoming my wife?'

I trembled, before breaking down.

'Yes,' I cried, my eyes fixed on the flashing red digits of an alarm clock in front of me. 'I can't imagine not being your wife.'

When I told my parents a few hours later, I was still crying. My mother touched my cheek, and said: 'May God always bless you.' She was so overcome, she couldn't even find the energy to call Aunt Jyoti.

My brother Anil got engaged a week later, to the lovely Lavina. I guessed he had been waiting for me all this time. We were all so joyful I thought we were going to burst. As if she didn't have enough to deal with, my mother couldn't help letting people know that Anand, too, would soon be 'ready'.

The first time my parents met Rohan was at the start of the parties for Anil and Lavina's wedding. He breezed into our home wearing an Indian silk outfit, and bent down to touch the feet of my father, and then my mother. My father hugged him, and said: 'Thank you for taking our daughter.'

Rohan beamed at him and said: 'Daddy, it's my very

great pleasure. And if I may say so, sir, it is also your very great loss.'

My brother, like all our cousins before him, had a typical Bombay wedding. Hundreds of people in a hotel ballroom, a week of festivities, a whirlwind of anonymous celebrants.

When it came time for Rohan and me to plan our wedding, we wanted the ceremonial as well as the sentimental. I had heard about a recently renovated Maharajah's palace, Ananda-in-the-Himalayas, an exquisite old edifice set in lush grounds. If we wanted a wedding that was to be soulful and spiritual, it could only be there.

When it's a girl's wedding, it doesn't matter if she's twenty or forty. I was as giddy and excited as I would have been had I been a teen-bride. So much so, that when a friend and I were compiling the guest-list, she reminded me that I had forgotten to include my fiancé.

'It would help if he were there,' she pointed out.

I had to take a month off from work to plan the wedding. (There is no way, ever, that an Indian bride can actually hold down a job while orchestrating her nuptials.) Marion didn't mind because she knew she'd be there, witnessing the thing she had been hearing about elliptically for years.

Everything had to be brought up from Delhi, a seven-hour car journey away. The bridal make-up artist came from the small, rural neighbouring town of Dehradun.

'Don't worry, madam,' she said, taking out something called 'Golly Glitter Blush' from her case. 'We do all the best weddings in Dehradun.'

There were truck-loads of flowers, hefty engraved silver furniture pieces, statues of deities, thousands of fairy lights and thick rolls of silk. Hundreds of cushions, yards upon yards of linens, boxes of silverware. There were maypoles, ottomans and pedestals. Enough to decorate a hundred acres of mountain property so that it would look like the scene of a jubilant Hindu wedding – or a movie set so elaborate that it made a Spielberg production resemble a kindergarten nativity play.

The holy River Ganges wound its sacred path far below, and we were so close to the heavens that I could reach out and touch the hand of Lord Shiva.

After all, I had to say thank you.

Epilogue

Rare as gold and from land of jade
Comes to him his beloved.
Though East and West be his to rule –
Anju still would be more precious

Had she pearls and rubies for her use
Content she could never be.
Where, oh where, has Rohan been –
Hearts linked now in unity.

Had they all life's treasures for their use
Content they could never be –
Come my love and unite with me –
And live now in harmony.

Merelika Shamash

Not long after my thirty-sixth birthday, Rohan and I stood beneath a full, luminescent moon surrounded by flickering flames and a million marigolds. I was wrapped in the sari my mother wore for her own wedding, forty years earlier; it was pale pink and encrusted with silver threads into which were woven the memories of a generation. Rohan led me around the nuptial fire, and I followed, our karmas cleansed by its warmth, our lives starting anew. Our families blessed us with their hands on our heads, and I cried the tears of a woman reborn.

He was exactly what everybody had in mind for me.

But by then it didn't even matter any more.